A Candlelight Ecstasy Romance®

"YOUR JOB IS TO KEEP MEN HAPPY, MS. FOSTER. AND I'M YOUR NEWEST PROSPECT."

"You know I don't run that kind of an escort service," Ellen said angrily. "You'll have to go elsewhere for the type of *servicing* you obviously have in mind."

"Servicing? Don't tell me that was a Freudian slip." Ellen turned bright red as Kane continued. "I know you don't like me, but you've been employed to make my stay in New York a success. Now I expect you to accompany me to a dinner party tonight. After that, we'll decide what to do next."

"That's impossible," she said haughtily. "I'll arrange for one of my assistants to go with you."

"I want *you*," Kane said grimly. "And I'm one customer who's going to get exactly what he wants."

CANDLELIGHT ECSTASY ROMANCES®

TONIGHT YOU'RE MINE

Edith Delatush

A CANDLELIGHT ECSTASY ROMANCE®

Published by
Dell Publishing Co., Inc.
1 Dag Hammarskjold Plaza
New York, New York 10017

Dell ® TM 681510, Dell Publishing Co., Inc.

Candlelight Ecstasy Romance®, 1,203,540, is a registered
trademark of Dell Publishing Co., Inc., New York, New York.

ISBN: 0-440-18988-8

Printed in the United States of America

April 1986

10 9 8 7 6 5 4 3 2 1

WFH

To Our Readers:

We have been delighted with your enthusiastic response to Candlelight Ecstasy Romances®, and we thank you for the interest you have shown in this exciting series.

In the upcoming months we will continue to present the distinctive sensuous love stories you have come to expect only from Ecstasy. We look forward to bringing you many more books from your favorite authors and also the very finest work from new authors of contemporary romantic fiction.

As always, we are striving to present the unique, absorbing love stories that you enjoy most—books that are more than ordinary romance. Your suggestions and comments are always welcome. Please write to us at the address below.

Sincerely,

The Editors
Candlelight Romances
1 Dag Hammarskjold Plaza
New York, New York 10017

CHAPTER ONE

"Will he be bringing his mistress with him again this time?"

Ellen Foster placed a check mark on the list she was studying before she raised her silvery blue eyes to her assistant. She didn't have to ask who Jeanne was referring to, but she remained deliberately vague as she tucked a stray auburn hair back into her sleek chignon.

"Who? Oh, you mean Kane Windsor. All I know is that he wants the same hotel suite that he had the last time. And remember, Jeanne, Miss Garcia is his *secretary*. Did you order those flame roses that she liked so much when she was here last time?"

Jeanne's sigh was dramatic. "Dozens. It isn't fair that one woman can look so devastatingly sultry and have a man like Kane Windsor too." She sighed again for effect. "And whatever label Miss Garcia might travel under, did you ever see anything as gorgeous as that diamond pendant he bought her?"

Ellen's lips tightened. She had been there a year ago when Rita Garcia was cooing over the necklace, and she had seen the sardonic lift of Kane Windsor's heavy eyebrows before he pulled out his checkbook. Yes, some women had everything.

"It's summer now, and you better check with Ralph that the air conditioner is working in the limousine. Mr. Lee tolerated the heat wave yesterday when I took him to the airport—he said Shanghai was worse—but I don't think Mr. Windsor will be that kind."

"You better believe it," Jeanne agreed fervently before eyeing her boss questioningly. "Do you still want me to pick him up at the airport?"

Ellen kept her expression blank. Jeanne had reason to ask. Ellen always smoothed the arrival of an account as important as Kane Windsor personally. And she knew the stakes in this visit were even higher. "Of course. I have full confidence in you."

Ellen watched approvingly as her assistant left with her own checklist. Jeanne Medrick, like the seven assistants in her employ, was hand-picked to look efficiently sophisticated. It was precisely the company image she wanted to project.

Her glance went to the letterhead on the sheaf of correspondence that her secretary had given her to sign, and she felt her pride surface: Foster Executive Services. Sometimes it was difficult to remember that only a little over a year ago she was still working at AR&S, the huge international conglomerate, as its protocol officer. This escort service had been only a dream then. Now she had contracts with several large banks and investment houses. It was her company's job to meet and pamper their clients, wealthy investors, whether foreign or from the States, when they visited New York City.

Foster Executive Services didn't end there. Its clients were in the income bracket that was used to demanding and having the best. It was Ellen's duty to see that, throughout their entire visit, they were coddled with reservations at the best restaurants and hotels and tickets to the best plays, even when none were available. Their wives or mistresses were given the same VIP treatment, with appointments to couturière houses and salons. At times, Ellen still could be stunned by the amount of money they spent.

Which brought her to Kane Windsor of Toronto, Canada. He had been her first client, and she'd been anxious to make sure that his visit went smoothly. Having the sleek but temperamental Rita Garcia—no matter what her position was—to cope with hadn't helped matters. By the time they had left, Ellen knew she could manage anything. Perhaps because her emotions had been so tense, the tall, ruggedly handsome man had lingered annoyingly in her memory. She told herself that she had given Jeanne this case in order to erase any unpleasant memories he might have retained about the way he had been handled during his previous visit.

"Ralph is here with the limousine," Jeanne announced from the door. "Are there any other orders before I go to LaGuardia and pick up Kane and friend? I bet she's the reason you dumped this on my lap. I dare say once is enough." She flashed a smirky grin before leaving.

They accepted that many of their clients were used to having servants and that they demanded instant attention, yet they found that most were considerate and easy to work with. Then occasionally there was a Rita Garcia, who expected immediate results from the smallest request. Ellen gave a sigh. Jeanne might demand a bonus, and she could well have earned one by the time Windsor's twelve-day visit was over.

It was two o'clock on Monday and Ellen had just finished dictating a report to Bella when Jeanne came into her office. Ellen looked up expectantly and immediately tensed when she saw her pale face.

"What happened?" she asked, further alarmed by the fact that Jeanne was avoiding looking at her.

"When you hear what I've done to our reputation,

you're probably going to ask for my resignation," Jeanne offered with a forced laugh. "It's unbelievable what gaffes I just pulled." She pushed her hand nervously through her black hair, destroying its carefully casual look.

"I was at the airport in plenty of time. From there, everything went downhill. Rita Garcia wasn't with our client. Instead, he was with an absolutely lovely blond woman. I cringed, thinking of those flaming roses waiting for them in the suite and how terribly wrong that color was for her pale peaches-and-cream complexion."

Jeanne heaved a dramatic sigh. "Ralph got the luggage without too long a wait. Thank goodness, because I managed to put my foot in my mouth on our way into the city. You know how we try to draw out the women on what they'd like to see while in town? So I gave my little talk, or started to. Mr. Windsor informed me in words carved out of ice that Ms. Agee was his secretary and that this was purely a business trip. Needless to say, I tried to find a hole in the upholstery so I could slide through and hide."

"With his track record, you weren't to know that this one was different," Ellen murmured consolingly as she saw the new contract with Little and Gower fly out the window.

Jeanne looked ill as she continued. She knew how important this particular job was to her boss. "But that isn't all. When we got to the hotel suite, I nearly died. The crazy florist got carried away. The rooms were blanketed in red roses. The place looked like a damn honeymoon bower! Windsor took one look and nearly exploded, and I can't say that I blame him. He said I had ten minutes to get the—I won't repeat the words he used—roses out of there. Believe me, I had all the bellhops there in minutes, and we practically threw

10

them out into the hall. I never want to see a rose again in my life!'' Her voice rose to an alarming wail.

Ellen forced a halt to the sinking feeling in her. "What then?" she asked resignedly, certain that the worst was yet to come.

"Somehow I remembered to call room service to make sure the special lunch we ordered was sent up, and I left." Jeanne's eyes were dark with apologies. Ellen was rousing herself to reassure her assistant that surely things weren't quite as bad as she had made them seem when the phone rang.

"Ms. Foster?" The voice could have frozen boiling water.

A knot formed in Ellen's middle, and she pressed a hand against it to ease the ache. "Yes, Mr. Windsor?" She didn't need to ask the man's identity.

"I would like to know who to thank for poisoning my secretary with that damn shrimp sauce on the fish. She went into allergic shock and has been rushed to the hospital." He ignored Ellen's small, helpless moan and continued. "I am without a secretary, and I need one immediately. I'm having a meeting in one hour. What do you plan to do about it?"

Ellen groaned as she sank back weakly against her chair.

"Is something wrong?" Bella asked anxiously, seeing her boss's stricken face.

Wrong? Her cherished dream of expansion seemed to lie shattered at her feet, and her secretary was asking if something was wrong. Thank heaven all the commitments for the expansion of her firm hadn't been made and only a few of the contracts had been signed!

"Are you there, Ms. Foster?" the voice of doom probed icily. "Am I to place my request to Little and Gower? I assume that your firm did at least see that a

11

limousine is available for my transportation, as you promised."

"Why, of course, Mr. Windsor." Her voice was a disgusting squeak, and she hurriedly cleared her throat. "Ralph is the chauffeur's name, and he has been informed of his duties."

"And the secretary?" Ice could never be as cold as that voice.

Ellen looked around wildly. Secretary? She could call the office help agency, but what guarantee had she that the person would meet his exacting demands? Her gaze rested on Bella, who was still looking anxiously at her, and she straightened in her chair. "A secretary is on her way, Mr. Windsor. I am certain she will meet all your requirements."

"We'll see."

The phone clicked in her ear at that doomsday pronouncement. Inhaling deeply to steady herself, Ellen turned to her secretary, hoping her smile didn't look as false as it felt. "Bella," she began.

Ellen felt like a traitor as she bundled Bella Carstairs into a taxi. She was a gem of a secretary and didn't deserve what Ellen had doubletalked her into doing. If anyone could salvage something from this horrible series of events, Bella could. One didn't send unsuspecting friends into a lion's den; but if anyone could come out of this relatively unscathed, Bella could. Maybe her blue-rinsed gray hair and sweet motherly face would soothe the savage beast. Ellen had seen Bella accomplish the impossible on several occasions, turning irritation into admiration and making friends for Foster Executive Services. She was counting heavily on her to do it now.

But meanwhile she was herself without Bella for the day. Ellen decided to check on Windsor's secretary to see how sick the shrimp sauce had made her. It was odd that no notification had been given to Foster of the change and that her name had not been forwarded to them. Was it because this English beauty was a last-minute replacement for the glamorous Ms. Garcia? She frowned. From Jeanne's description of the woman, Kane Windsor seemed to like variety in his traveling companions.

Ellen had to call the hotel first to get the secretary's name and to find what hospital she had been taken to. One would think that Windsor's office would have given her that information, she thought irritably. They'd been flooded with plenty of other information about which restaurants he preferred and what plays he wanted to see.

"What's the news?" Jeanne asked, seeing Ellen's concerned expression when the calls were finished.

"He has reason to be angry," Ellen admitted worriedly. "They're keeping Frances Agee under observation overnight in the intensive care unit."

Jeanne was aghast. "Oh, no! Will she be all right? You know, when we went over the menu, nobody mentioned anything about a shrimp sauce on the fish." The threat of a possible lawsuit was on both of their minds.

Ellen grimaced. "I checked with the chef. It seems he wanted a hint of extra flavoring and used some water that he'd cooked some shrimp in. Being highly allergic, that was all she needed."

"I've heard of cases like that. What do we do now?"

"We'll have to see that she gets the best of care. I know hospitals allow only the family to visit while patients are in intensive care, but once she's out I'll have to go and see what I can do to mend fences. Meanwhile, will you see that the hospital bills come here?" Lord only knew what they would amount to!

Jeanne left to use her phone, and Ellen rested her

head tiredly on her hand. Kane Windsor had barely managed to control his temper and disgust. She could imagine how the Little and Gower investment house was reacting just about now to his report on what they'd consider her shocking ineptitude.

She'd spent months trying to convince Little and Gower that her company's services were just what they needed, and Windsor had been offered to her as a test case. Based on their agreement to give her a try and on her confidence that a lucrative contract was as good as signed, she had advanced the date for the proposed expansion of her business to Atlanta and Dallas. As a result, Ellen was faced with a multitude of additional expenses now. She was getting what she deserved for being so foolhardy. Just because her success in the past year had surpassed all her expectations, she had thought she was invincible. Humble pie time started as of now.

She pulled out the folders for the two proposed additions. She'd gone through endless interviews before signing on the prospective managers, and now she had to tell them that the offices might not open for a while, if at all. She wondered how reasonable they'd be if she were forced to let them go.

Her primary concern was that the character of her employees be morally impeccable. She was fully aware of the smirking leers at parties when her company was under discussion. *Escort service, eh? Wonder how much* her *services cost, and if she's worth it!*

She was sensitive on the subject, and with good cause. Three months ago, she had had to let a promising assistant go. Peggy Delancey had broken a firm ruling by succumbing to advances from a client. It was weeks of waiting for repercussions before Ellen could breathe easily again. One scandal could destroy her company.

As a result of that incident, she was now forced to be extra careful about the reputations of those who worked for her. Fraternizing was strictly forbidden. Under no circumstance were any of her employees allowed to date a client. It was a strong selling point when she negotiated contracts with banks and investment houses. In fact, several of her clients had a clause inserted that stated their contracts could be terminated if the rule were broken.

She wound a loose strand of auburn hair around her finger, a nervous gesture she had begun in childhood. The Little and Gower contract would never reach the signing phase now, once Kane Windsor unloaded his complaints.

"Ellen . . ."

Jeanne stood in the doorway, her face stricken, and the knot in Ellen's stomach tightened.

"I don't think I want to hear what you have to say," she replied grimly.

"The ticket agent just called. The tickets that we ordered for Mr. Windsor for *La Cage aux Folles* aren't."

"Aren't what?" Ellen felt the blood drain from her face. "But he promised he had them!"

"There's a big VIP party in town, and the government requisitioned them. He had to give them up."

Ellen swore, causing Jeanne to blink in disbelief. She'd never heard any off-color words from her boss, not even in the beginning, when they had been under the constant strain wondering if her dream would succeed.

For a moment, Ellen's eyes closed as if she were in pain. Then her shoulders squared, and she began issuing orders. Considering the popularity of the play, the effort would be a waste of time but she had to make it. "Get everyone who's here to call all the ticket agencies in town to see if there are any available. If not, put a

15

hold on two tickets for every play that's on. Then say a prayer for me. It looks like I have a big selling job to do. I'm going to have to beard the lion in his den and convince him that a substitute play will suit him fine."

She smiled grimly when she saw sympathy on Jeanne's face before the woman hurried to do her bidding. Her glance went to the square chrome clock on her desk. Bella should be calling soon to tell her that Windsor's meeting was over. Then her time of trial would start.

Her hand found the stray hair again, and she tugged at it with a feeling of resignation. She'd done everything possible to avoid meeting this man during his stay, but it looked as if the fates had outmaneuvered her on every count.

CHAPTER TWO

Jeanne reported the results of her canvassing of the ticket agencies. As expected, there was nothing available for the sellout Broadway play, and she had been only partially successful in getting two seats together at the other popular ones.

"Make me a list of the ones you have," Ellen replied, dumping two aspirin into her palm before she reached for her mug of lukewarm coffee. She didn't know which was worse, the throbbing in her head or the knot twisting her stomach.

When Bella finally called, her opening statement did little to ease the tension. "I thought *you* kept my nose to the grindstone, but, Madame, Kane Windsor has you beat. If I didn't love you dearly, and if he weren't such a handsome son-of-a-gun, I'd say take all these reports and stuff them you know where."

"Where are you calling from?"

"Little and Gower. They gave me a cubbyhole and a typewriter so that I could type Mr. Windsor's notes. He wants them first thing in the morning."

"I expected you to come here and do them."

"Honey, Mr. Windsor okayed their offer, and when he speaks, I listen. Besides, you should see this terrific new typewriter I'm using. It does everything but make coffee. I'm trying to figure out how I can abscond with it tucked in my pocketbook."

17

Ellen gave a grim chuckle. Bella's mammoth-size pocketbooks were a joke in the office. They were constantly amazed over what she kept in them. "Then you didn't find him to be too impossible to work for?" To date, nothing had fazed her unflappable secretary, but remembering his anger, she was afraid even Bella might have folded.

"Let's just say I should be nominated for sainthood. I think his secretary chickened out and took the coward's way out. But I must say, there is something about him. Now, if I were fifteen years younger . . ."

An image flashed immediately before Ellen: a broad forehead underlined by a dark slash of eyebrows, black eyes that seemed capable of looking through one and beyond, lips firm and finely drawn, and a chin that looked as if it had been hewn from granite. It was a rugged, forceful face, and she was surprised that she could remember it in such detail after a year's time. Oh, yes. She could relate to what Bella was inferring.

"Well, I won't keep you from your work. We'll see you tomorrow," Ellen replied.

Bella hesitated, and Ellen rested her head resignedly on her hand. "Er—it seems Mr. Windsor expects me to work for him for his entire visit. He called the doctor who's taking care of Miss Agee and found out that she'll be staying in the hospital for a few days for further observation. It seems her reaction caused fluid to form in her lungs. I think Mr. Windsor plans to send her home to recuperate when she's finally discharged. Look, I'm caught up with everything in the office, and I'm certain Sue can cope until I come back."

Sue was the office typist. She'd have to tell the others to go easy on the woman until this ever-deteriorating fiasco was over. "Don't worry, we'll manage. Just don't let Mr. Windsor get to you."

"I should be so lucky!" Bella chuckled. "You should

18

see the young things here falling over themselves. He's so sublimely indifferent to their fawning that I have to laugh. I guess he has a bigger and better prize waiting for him tonight."

Which reminded Ellen forcibly of the distasteful chore ahead of her. "Do you know if he's gone back to the hotel? I have to see him about some business."

"I believe so. He said something about several calls he had to make. And you're right, I'd better get on with my work, or I'll be here until midnight."

Ellen went to the bathroom to check her appearance. After all that had gone wrong, the image she needed to project was one of calm assurance. Thank goodness she'd worn her new raw silk suit. The teal blue was perfect with the rich auburn color of her hair and gave an accent to her silver blue eyes.

It was while she was reapplying the lipstick that she had chewed off during the day's frustration that Ellen realized Bella had said nothing about Kane reporting her less-than-perfect service to Little and Gower. Could it be that the contract was still salvageable?

Fat chance, she corrected herself morosely as she flagged down a cruising taxi. Just wait until Kane heard the reason for her showing up! By the time the taxi deposited her in midtown at the Plaza, she was resigned to facing the full force of his anger once he had her in his power.

In his power? The unexpected phraseology disturbed her, but then she reached the front desk and the thought was replaced by irritation. It was impossible to notify Mr. Windsor of her arrival because his phone was busy. After fretting for half an hour, and after further attempts proved to be fruitless, Ellen decided to take matters into her own hands. It was approaching six o'clock, and her stomach was telling her it needed more than the endless cups of coffee that had kept her going since breakfast. Once she escaped, she intended to go to her favorite restaurant and have a tall, relaxing drink before pampering herself with the most expensive item on the menu. She deserved it after the day she had just lived through.

She had the switchboard operator try one more time. When she found that Windsor's line was still busy, she went to the tier of elevators and punched the number of his floor. His suite number was engraved on her mind: Hadn't she made the reservation, careful that it was the best? As soon as her shock had passed when Little and Gower had given her Kane Windsor's name, she'd taken on the challenge to personally guarantee a smooth ten-day stay for him. She was doing it, she told herself, to compensate for any inadequacy he might have noticed in her handling of him during his visit a year ago. It was important to her that he remember her company in glowing terms. The Canadian market was as yet untouched, and she had hoped he'd be a beginning. Oh, well.

To steady her nerves, she inhaled deeply several times before knocking at the door of his suite. A loud "Come in, the door is unlocked" startled her. Toronto must be the Promised Land if he didn't feel it necessary to lock doors.

The elevator down the hall opened, and a waiter stepped out, carrying a tray. Ellen realized the reason for the open door. Mr. Windsor had evidently ordered coffee and had left it unlocked so he wouldn't be disturbed while making his calls.

She followed the waiter into the room. He had said come in, hadn't he? A handsome burled maple desk sat between two windows that framed views of Central Park. Kane hugged the phone to his ear with his shoulder as he flipped through a black notebook and jotted down some figures. He pointed absently to the cocktail table, indicating where the tray should be placed. Only then did he notice her.

A fractional lift of a black eyebrow was his only reaction to her presence as he argued figures with whomever he was talking to. Ellen moved several portfolios aside so the waiter could put down his burden. He smiled at the tip she gave him and left quietly.

His dark eyes remained fastened on her, but Ellen refused to let that fluster her. With surprisingly steady hands, she poured coffee into a china cup. Recalling his preference, she added a little cream. Now why had that piece of information remained with her? She hadn't seen Windsor in a year. She placed the cup and saucer within easy reach, and the subtle scent of his expensive aftershave lotion enveloped her with a gentle pull. That scent was an integral part of her memory of him, and it triggered a recall of the nervousness that came over her whenever she had been near him during that fateful three-day visit.

The suite had been reserved for two, and the kitchen had included two cups on the tray. Kane thanked her with a nod before waving a finger imperiously at the silver pot, indicating she should help herself. She did, and sank into a soft chair. The coffee cup occupied her hands while he continued on the phone If only he'd stop staring at her with those jet eyes that seemed to see everything but that gave away no secrets!

Kane had discarded his jacket on the sofa, and he'd loosened his tie and opened the top few buttons of his shirt. In Ellen's memories, his tall, muscular form was always dressed to sartorial perfection. This new, relaxed man did unsettling things to her already-churning stomach. To banish his image, she deliberately examined the room. It was of a comfortable size, and

21

she knew that the doors, at opposite sides, opened to private bed and bath suites.

The hotel had gone through a recent renovation. Ellen approved of the elegance of the French provincial decor. She was trying to decide if its blue wallpaper would do in her living room when she heard Kane hang up the phone.

His gaze remained fastened on her over the cup as he slowly drank the coffee. The silence lengthened as he deliberately drew out that simple act. She gave him high marks for dramatizing the situation. Tension pulled on her nerves, but she decided to wait him out. He was a master at taking command of a situation, but she wasn't going to let him intimidate her.

He placed the cup onto the saucer with careful attention and returned to the desk with equal consideration. He then rose and came to stand a threatening three feet from where she sat. "So we meet again, Ms. Foster. It took you long enough to get here!"

Ellen blinked once and stared at him in surprise while trying to understand his meaning. She could read nothing in his expression, yet she felt she was being subtly threatened. For heaven's sake, this wasn't the Middle Ages, when a lord could resort to beatings for inept services!

A lord? What fanciful flight was her imagination taking? She gave herself a mental shake even as she found it easy to imagine him standing like that in some stone castle with his long muscular legs spread aggressively apart, his face hard and unforgiving, as some recalcitrant servant stood quaking before him waiting to be sentenced.

She inhaled deeply. "I came to apologize for any inconvenience you've had, Mr. Windsor," she began with what she hoped was the proper conciliatory tone.

"*Any* inconvenience, Ms. Foster?" he interrupted

coldly. "My secretary goes into anaphylactic shock and stops breathing because of food that you ordered, and you hope I haven't been inconvenienced? Don't tell me you're planning some other catastrophic event for me that would make what has already happened seem like a mere inconvenience?"

Ellen pressed her hand against her stomach to ease the sudden pain. "I'm sorry. I had no idea that her reaction was that severe." Tired of being constantly on the defensive where this man was concerned, she nourished a sudden spurt of anger. She rose, not wanting to have to talk up to him. "However, we are not clairvoyant. If someone had thought enough ahead to notify my office of her allergies, this would never have happened."

She was tall and stood almost six feet in her heels, which was just inches shorter than he was. He stared for long seconds at the fire lighting her silvery eyes before his gaze dropped to the rapid rise and fall that her agitation gave to her breasts. The corners of his mouth depressed as if with an inner smile of satisfaction before he turned and took a step away. Relieved to have the extra space between them, Ellen didn't care to probe into what was behind his smile.

"At least the last report is that she's responding to treatment," he informed her.

"I know. I called to check. As soon as she's well enough to have visitors, I plan to see her."

He nodded briefly. "I should thank you for finding Ms. Carstairs on such short notice. She's been a big help so far."

Her eyebrow arched. *A compliment? From Kane Windsor?* "I have every confidence in Bella. She's my secretary."

He looked taken aback by the information. "I didn't

23

realize that. She should have said something when I told her that I wanted her until I left."

"So she informed me," Ellen admitted drily. "Since I feel somewhat responsible for your predicament, I told her to continue with you. I can manage with my other help until you leave."

He eased his long frame onto the sofa and looked at her quizzically as if trying to decipher something about her. "That's very generous of you."

The tension between them had dispersed, and Ellen sank back into her chair with a sigh of relief. For the first time, she noticed traces of exhaustion on his face. Sympathy surged in her. He must have suffered through a harrowing time when his secretary collapsed. And on top of that, whatever business he was negotiating with Little and Gower must be taking considerable concentration. The man deserved whatever relaxation he could get.

Only then did she remember her reason for coming, and her hand went automatically to press on her stomach. At the moment he was at rest, but she wasn't fooled. The volcano was dormant, not extinguished. What would the next explosion be like? After the day she'd put in because of all the fiascos that had happened since his arrival, she didn't think she could handle it.

"I, er, came to discuss something with you." She hesitated, seeing his expression harden slightly. He'd have her hyperventilating soon if she kept sucking in breaths in an effort to calm her nerves. "It's about the show we booked for you this evening," she explained bravely. "All the spare tickets have been requisitioned for a VIP party, and we were informed that the ones being held for you were in the group."

When he gave no response, she continued nervously. "We were able to get pairs for several other

24

shows. When you select one, we'll simply adjust the dates."

"I must explain something to you, Ms. Foster. One of the ways I bribe my secretaries into taking these trips with me is to give them the added perk of seeing Broadway shows."

She stared at him dumbfounded. Did he really think they had to be bribed? Hadn't he ever looked in a mirror? He even had Bella falling into a swoon.

"They also provide me with a convenient companion, since I don't like going by myself. Now that you've eliminated Ms. Agee from filling that position, I expect you to provide a substitute."

Ellen stiffened. "I don't run that type of escort service," she reminded him curtly. "You'll have to go elsewhere for that kind of servicing."

His smile was feral. "Servicing? For shame, Ms. Foster. Was that a Freudian slip?"

Ellen felt the heat rise to her face, and she was aghast. She hadn't blushed since she was seven, when her father had happened upon her behind the garage, where the neighbor's boy was attempting his—and her —first kiss.

He regarded her flushed face with intense interest. "I haven't had a blind date for years. I'm very selective. Which brings me to this problem confronting us. Tell me, Ms. Foster, are you busy tonight?"

Ice shards replaced the silver in her eyes. "It's a firm policy that anyone employed by Foster Executive Services never fraternizes with the clients."

His smile became more feral and his voice took on a velvet quality. "Most admirable. But we aren't talking about fraternizing. You can forget about the theater tonight. My request is for you to accompany me to this dinner party I've been invited to by a business acquaintance."

Seeing her refusal form, he decided to lean harder. "My secretary always comes with me on these occasions. She's quite good at evaluating people and frequently comes up with interesting observations that I can use later. I guess it's very much like what you do in your business, hmm?"

"It's impossible," she seethed. Who did he think he was with his manipulating!

He rose, and Ellen hurriedly stood up too, her chin high in defiance. "Tut tut, Ms. Foster. All I want is your charming company tonight. Certainly that's not too much to ask when you consider what I've had to put up with today. Not to mention what Frances is suffering." He reached for his black book and clicked his pen. "Now, your address, please."

Ellen amazed herself by complying. But what alternative did she have? She was deeply committed to her expansion, and he'd been kind enough not to mention to Little and Gower the less-than-impressive service he'd received so far.

And she couldn't fault him on his reason for making his request. Through an absurd series of events, she was indirectly responsible for his being without his secretary—in whatever function she filled.

"I'll be there at seven-thirty," he told her.

Furious over the trap she found herself in, she stalked past him to reach the door. Her one thought was to escape in order to regroup. He tossed his book onto the table and followed her. A surprisingly strong finger that curled under her chin effectively halted her flight.

"I had a very trying day. While business discussions usually find their way into these affairs, I intend to relax." He gazed long into the stony face that was raised to his, and his expression softened. "I guess

26

your day has been hectic, too. Shall we call a truce and simply enjoy ourselves?"

He smiled, and his teeth gleamed white in contrast to his deeply tanned complexion. Ellen blinked at the change such a simple exercise of muscles made on his stern face. "You're a very lovely lady. Will you please me and wear something outlandishly feminine tonight?"

A sigh caught in her throat. Brother! When he turned it on, she doubted that there was a woman alive who could resist his magnetism.

His thumb moved slowly over her full lower lip, and it was several seconds before Ellen was conscious of the seduction being performed. Feeling smothered by too much Kane Windsor, she jerked her head from its restraint and gave him a telling glare. Feeling oddly unable to speak, she turned to leave. He reached past her, opened the door, and watched her proud walk as she went to the elevator.

He wore a thoughtful expression as the door closed. He had no idea why he had come down so hard on her in the beginning, except that her unexpected arrival had set off an odd need to reject her intrusion in his life. But everything had changed when he saw her blush. When was the last time he'd seen that enticing phenomenon in a woman?

His hand pushed roughly through his thick black hair. It wasn't the smoothest opening gambit that he'd ever tried on a woman who intrigued him, but it was the best he could come up with considering the circumstances. At least he had her agreeing to go out with him that evening. He had twelve days to see what made the elegant Ms. Foster tick.

CHAPTER THREE

The taxi careened to a halt in front of Ellen's apartment complex. She gave a forced smile to Bernie, the evening security guard, as he hurried to open the door for her. As she ascended in the elevator, the tip of her tongue dampened her lower lip. She was uncomfortably aware that she'd been doing that all through the ride, as if in an effort to cool the throbbing heat she felt.

She didn't select her wardrobe until she'd taken several antacids to ease her unhappy stomach and had relaxed her tense muscles under the pulsing spray of the shower. Only then did she remove the black cocktail dress from its plastic cover. He wanted something feminine, did he? The last time she had worn this gown, her escort had hyperventilated throughout the evening.

On the hanger it seemed a simple dress, but once it was on her body it took on a whole new character. The spaghetti straps exposed creamy shoulders that begged for caresses. The casual drape to the bodice somehow brought attention to what it shielded. The risqué side slit to the slim skirt exposed a long, slender thigh. But it was when she walked that the dress really proved to be a masterpiece in design. The shiny black silk undulated with each step, casting mysterious shadows and highlights that teased and hypnotized the eye.

A midnight blue eyeshadow added attention to the remarkable silver blue of her eyes. She applied a deep red lipstick and a top coating of silver pink that gave added lushness to the full curves of her lips. Since her escort was tall enough to take the extra height she swept her thick hair into a loose knot on top of her head, with a few strands coaxed loose to bring attention to her long, slender neck.

After slipping into thin-strapped sandals, Ellen examined herself critically in the mirror. She nodded approvingly at her tall, slender image. She projected just the right mixture of sophistication and femininity. What wasn't obvious was the passion implicit in the full curve of her lips. The tumble of hair invited male fingers to release the loose knot and bury themselves in the clinging softness.

Finishing a few minutes before Kane's arrival, Ellen found herself nervously pacing her living room. Annoyed by her own reaction, she tried to concentrate on the assortment of mail she'd tossed onto the cocktail table, but her attention remained on the man she was to spend the evening with.

It had been a long time since anyone, far less a man who seemed as consistently threatening as Kane, had managed to talk her into doing something she didn't want to do. To her disgust, she had to admit that her irritation was tinged with admiration at his adroit manipulation. She had to admit he'd easily won their game of one-upmanship, but the next round would be hers.

Ellen didn't investigate her own insidious conviction that there'd be more occasions besides this evening. Reason dictated that after tonight he'd have time to find a replacement. Anyone like Kane Windsor would have no trouble filling the rest of his free time with willing companions. No, his evenings would not be lonely—or without whatever "servicing" he desired.

She cringed as she remembered the embarrassment. Had she really been so crass as to suggest such a thing? It had been an instinctive reaction, a lashing out brought on by her resentment over how the uninformed frequently regarded her escort service, but that didn't excuse her, she admitted. She tossed the unopened mail back onto the table and resumed pacing.

She had to bring her emotions under firm control before Kane arrived. Whenever he was near, all her systems automatically went into a high gear that was disconcerting. The phenomenon wasn't new; it had occurred a year ago too. Then she'd assumed that it was because he was her first client, and she had felt that the success of her new company depended on whatever report he gave to the bank that had hired her.

In spite of the series of recent events, which would have put a saint on edge, the same undercurrent of emotion had returned the moment she stepped into his hotel room. She deserved a prize for having performed rationally under his relentless stare. There was no getting away from it: Kane Windsor had the ability to make her feel all too uncomfortable. So how was she going to handle a whole evening with him?

Very carefully. The answer to the old joke caused her to smile slightly. Admittedly she owed him this evening, but she intended to be firm in telling him that after this he had to find someone else to fill in for his secretary. Thank goodness this was a private dinner party. It eliminated the possibility that anyone from Little and Gower would catch her breaking her strict rule about nonfraternization, a rule they heartily approved of.

Her introspection was brought to an abrupt halt when the security phone rang and Bernie announced Kane's arrival. When she heard the elevator stop at her floor, Ellen opened the door for him and promptly found herself clinging to it for a breathless second. He demanded attention in a business suit, but in a white tuxedo top, he was absolutely awe-inspiring. Not that he was good-looking; that would be too insipid a description of this forceful man. For the first time, she wondered if there were Indian blood in his background that gave him the swarthy complexion, the harsh angles to his face, the dark piercing eyes.

And they were piercing now. They started at the coil on top of her head and traveled with leisurely appreciation to her elegant shoes. He missed nothing, she was certain, on the way.

"Now that's what I call dynamite." His smile was pure approval.

Her lashes lowered quickly before he caught the extent of her own approval. "This is the sort of dress you requested, isn't it?"

He laughed. "Yes, but I never dreamed my fantasy would come to such vivid life."

She smiled thinly, absurdly pleased with his compliment. She led him into the apartment, acutely aware of his subtle aroma wafting around her. "I'll get my purse if you want to leave, or do you have time for a drink?"

He didn't answer at once, and she glanced over her shoulder at him in question. His eyes held dark smoky lights as he watched with rapt attention the way the silk material glided over her supple body with each step. "Fascinating!" he murmured in frank admiration before replying to her question. "We have time for a short drink. What do you suggest?"

Ellen moved to the black lacquered Chinese cabinet that opened into a bar. "Will a vodka martini do?"

"Excellent," he answered abstractly, his attention focusing on the large room.

She concentrated on the measurements, wondering what he thought of the decor. The building was old, but the charm was in the extra-large rooms that one couldn't find in modern apartments. He'd never know the frustration and time she'd spent before arriving at that exact light apricot shade for the walls. The fruitless hunt for a deeper tone for the thick plush carpet had ended only by having it dyed to her specification. Each piece of furniture had been an adventure in discovery that was still going on. She'd found the perfect desk for the bay window only recently in an antique shop, but unfortunately, the price was more than she could afford at the moment.

"Who prunes your forest?" he asked. A pair of weeping ficus trees bracketed the large bay window and almost touched the twelve-foot ceiling. He examined them with amused amazement.

She handed him the thin-stemmed crystal before eyeing the graceful trees critically. "I never cared for hanging plants, but I do like greenery in a room. Considering these dimensions, I needed something strong enough to make a statement. Do you think they're taking over?"

"Let's put it this way. I wouldn't be surprised to discover a pair of birds taking up housekeeping in them."

She met his humor with a smile. "It's an interesting idea. Do you think I should go in for canaries or parakeets?"

He examined the pastel carpeting and the white textured sofa and chairs with the pillows in solid slashes of color. "Somehow I don't think they'd go with this room," he conceded drily.

"You have something there. Besides, I don't believe in caging birds, or animals for that matter. They have a right to their freedom."

He looked thoughtfully at her while tasting his drink. "You've created a charming room. You're a very exciting woman, and I'm surprised at the calm, the serenity you've achieved here. Is this a part of you that you keep hidden?" His gaze swept the room again before his dark eyes rested on her once more. "I wonder what else is hidden behind that veneer of sophistication?"

Oh, no you don't! The last thing she was interested in was a come-on from him. Ellen placed her empty glass on a side table and reached for her black silk purse. "Shall I call down to the guard to flag a taxi for us? We don't want to be late."

Her chin rose to a defiant angle. She was thirty, and it was a long time since she'd permitted any probing into the private part of her life.

"What do you want me to do?" Ellen asked in the cab, after Kane had given the address to the driver.

"Do?" he asked as he settled back into the seat.

Ellen shifted defensively to the window. He wasn't a massive man, yet he seemed to fill the interior of the taxi completely. "Perhaps I should reword that. Is there anyone special I should pay attention to? You said one of Ms. Agee's duties was to check out possible business connections. I'm not along to just occupy space."

"But you do that so beautifully," he protested silkily. A large, muscular hand enclosed hers, but she gave him a sardonic look and pulled free. "The party is being given by Arthur and Lydia Bigelow. He's a big

33

customer of one of Windsor's companies, and when he heard I was coming to New York, he insisted I attend."

"Which company is that?" She knew that Windsor Enterprises was family owned and that it had several diverse companies under that blanket name.

"Windsor Cardboard. We have several pulp mills, and they process paper as well as cardboard. Bigelow is one of the largest packaging manufacturers in the country. The fancy box that held the last dress you bought could well have been made by him, as well as the heavy-duty crating for your office furniture."

"Do you know who else will be there?"

He gave a faint shrug. "There's a convention on packaging going on at the Coliseum, but I don't know if he's inviting any of his competitors."

Recalling the myriad types of cardboard one comes across routinely, from posterboard to thick corrugated boxes, she could imagine the importance of the convention. "Does your company have a booth there?" she questioned.

"Naturally. That's one reason why I'm here now. I decided to combine that with seeing Little and Gower."

It made sense. And because she always found other people's lines of work interesting, she asked more about his company. Windsor Cardboard was evidently a new acquisition, and one he'd pushed for. She was shortly swamped with phrases such as *kraft pulping, cellulose content,* and *chemical bleaching processes* that had her searching madly through forgotten science lectures to bring sense to his words.

Seeing her struggle to keep abreast of his discourse, he gave a dry chuckle. "You started it," he accused. "Never ask a man about a subject near and dear to him. The company was floundering, but I could see all sorts of potential, and I talked the home office into buying it. In retaliation, the Board—and that means my father—dumped the mess onto my lap. It's my baby now, and the challenge is mine. As a result, I'm pretty immersed in getting the factory back onto its feet."

This time when he captured her hand, she didn't pull away. His breath was a warm benediction on her wrist as he brushed a kiss on her palm. "That's for listening with such forebearance," he murmured.

The huskiness in his voice sent an electric shiver of awareness down Ellen's spine. A small rent appeared in her barricade, and she was thankful when the taxi drew to a stop.

They were in the east sixties. The stone building had been built in the same era as her own apartment, and Ellen looked forward with interest to seeing if the rooms were similar.

The Bigelow apartment occupied the whole top floor. He'd bought two apartments, Arthur Bigelow boomed when he saw her interest, and had knocked the walls out. After all, a man had to breathe.

And he needed that space. He was an immense man, six foot six and well over two hundred fifty pounds of solid muscle. He'd started out as a lumberjack and had worked his way up, he announced proudly with a voice that once must have made trees shake.

Ellen was in awe of so much contained power until she saw the gentleness that came into his eyes when he looked at his wife. Lydia was a full-busted woman with thick blond braids circling her head. My God, Ellen gaped irreverently, when they came together, more than trees would shake!

When she spied the suppressed laughter in Kane's face, she wondered if he had latched on to her outrageous whimsey. "Awe-inspiring, aren't they?" he agreed after he gave their drink orders to the waiting maid. "The story goes that on their honeymoon, they finally gave up fixing the bed and left the mattress on the floor."

Ellen choked on the canapé she was swallowing. His expression was properly solicitous as he patted her back. "I'll get you for that," she gasped.

His grin was unrepenting as he popped a caviar-topped cracker into his mouth. Over two dozen people were wandering through the apartment, and he examined them to see if there were any he recognized. "It looks like Bigelow has invited some of his competitors," he admitted, which brought Ellen back to his reason for bringing her here.

The buffet dinner was superb. Listening to the conversation going on around her, Ellen guessed that a good part of Bigelow's task force at the convention was also at the party. Kane was pigeonholed by two men, and she wandered off when the talk turned immediately to business. As she passed other groups, she heard the same phrases that Kane had used in the taxi, as well as others such as *graphic takes, color imprint,* and *pressure and heat tests.* The convention must have been a success. The talk was animated, centering on the new ideas and techniques that had been presented.

And then a new guest arrived, and panic sent her heart into an uncomfortable double beat. What in the world was Thomas Gower doing here? Once he saw her with Kane, she could say good-bye to any hopes for her contract.

Frantic seconds passed before she could think clearly again. Lydia and Arthur Bigelow were at the door greeting Gower and Florence, his wife. It was evident that the two had just arrived and that her presence here with their client was still unknown. Relief flooded her, leaving her momentarily weak, and she leaned against a chair for support.

Gower was the junior member of the investment company. From the few meetings Ellen had had with him, she suspected that the strict code that the company insisted upon came from Archibald Little, the senior partner, who was Gower's father-in-law. Her gaze shifted curiously to the woman with him.

Recalling the woman's father, she was startled to see how closely she resembled him. Like Archibald Little, Florence Little Gower was painfully thin, with an austere expression. He, however, still wore, of all things, pince-nez glasses that pinched the high bridge of his nose. Yet they didn't camouflage the piercing intensity of his pale blue eyes. Ellen remembered his lips, which had seemed locked in a permanent disapproving purse. His attitude about modern morality was well known and was the butt of many jokes on Wall Street. He had proved to be a very uncomfortable man to deal with.

Mrs. Gower couldn't deny her heritage. Being a woman, she was a slightly more gentle version of her father, but not much. Had she been programmed with the same strict Victorian outlook? If so, Ellen felt sorry for her husband. Poor Thomas Gower mustn't get much fun out of life. Not only did he have to give lip service to her father's ideology in the office, but then he had no relief when he got home. Perhaps his outlet was in the excitement of making money, and that was compensation enough for him.

The massive forms of the Bigelows bracketed the new arrivals as they ushered them into the room. Her panic resurged, and Ellen looked around frantically for Kane. He was still in conversation and unaware of the newcomers. Would he appreciate the full extent of what the arrival of the Gowers meant? With escape

37

paramount in her mind, she turned and forced herself not to run as she sought sanctuary through the glass doors behind her.

The terrace was wide and looked south along Third Avenue toward the spiky skyline of lower Manhattan. Few people were braving the chill that was carried on the evening breeze. Ellen drew in deep breaths, thankful for the cool touch on her hot face. For the moment, she was safe.

What a fool she'd been! she seethed in rising disgust. How could she have let that Canadian talk her into going along with his wishes? How could she have permitted one moment of weak compliance to threaten all that she worked so hard for? She thought of all the long hours of work and stress, the frustrations and triumphs that had brought Foster Executive Services to where it was at present. What hold did Kane Windsor have over her that had made her do something so foolish?

The terrace was on the tenth floor, and she went to stand by the railing. It was several minutes before her temper cooled enough for her to be able to admire the colorful scene spread before her. Whatever stars were in the velvet sky conceded victory to the competition from the multicolored man-made lights that lay like a sparkling carpet at her feet.

"Impressive, isn't it?"

Her nerves tightened in alarm before she glanced at the man coming to the railing to stand beside her. For a horrible moment she thought Thomas Gower had followed her to—what? Damn her with accusation? It wasn't like her to be this paranoid. "I've seen it after a rain, and it's twice as brilliant with the lights reflecting from the wet pavement."

They contemplated the view in shared silence for several minutes before she turned to look at him. He was slender and as tall as she, and he had a long sensitive face. "I take it you're in packaging also," she murmured. It was hardly a guess, and the man laughed.

"Yes, and I'm one of the competitors." His laugh turned self-deprecatory. "Actually, I can hardly call myself that. My company is so small, Bigelow probably considers me no more annoying than a mosquito."

She liked the way his long face crinkled when he laughed. "What is your line?" she asked.

"I manufacture specialty packaging, which means the orders are too small for Bigelow to bother with. That means that I'm safe doing my little thing without being squashed. To fill my clients' needs, I have to find companies that are willing to produce small quantities of highly specialized paper without charging an arm and a leg. That's one of the reasons I'm here at the convention."

Recalling Kane's similar enthusiasm, Ellen stilled a smile as the man continued earnestly to talk about the problems his search entailed. She couldn't help but recall her own enthusiasm during those first months whenever anyone had asked her about her own business.

"I think I might know someone who can help you," she offered when he paused to light a cigarette. "Do you have a business card with you?"

He was sliding one out of his wallet when a shadow fell over them. Turning, she saw Kane blocking the light from the door. He seemed perfectly relaxed, but she sensed anger, and she stared questioningly at him.

"You've come at the perfect moment," she announced after a hurried glance at the card in her hand. "Kane, I want you to meet Miles Walker. Mr. Walker, this is Kane Windsor of Windsor Cardboard. He might be able to help you with your problem."

The men shook hands, and Miles gave a quick rundown of his requirements. Kane's hand rested on the railing, trapping her beside him. She was acutely conscious of how her shoulder brushed his chest with every breath he drew. The ornate iron prevented her from moving away from his aggressive possessiveness. Why he was acting possessively, she had no idea. Certainly Kane had no reason to warn off Miles Walker! Their meeting had been purely accidental and was certainly no cause for him to be angry.

Other men had tried the hands-off bit with her, and she had soon set them straight. She was her own person. No one dictated her moves.

Kane's tantalizing scent was carried by the breeze and wrapped her in its enchanting aroma. His body warmth became a subtle stimulation, as his chest brushed sensuously against her. His firmness spoke of hard muscles and a well-tuned male body. A tingling started deep within her; the strength of her response caught her unawares.

The men shook hands again, with a promise from Kane to call the next day at his office. Ellen breathed a sigh of relief when Kane stepped away. He suggested they leave, and he guided her from the terrace. She was acutely conscious of his fingers burning little brands into the small of her back. Somehow she managed to stop their forward movement before they entered the room, and she told him of the Gowers' arrival.

He frowned as he listened to her hurried explanation. "So that's why you disappeared out here. Don't you think you're overreacting a little? This is the twentieth century, woman. No company can exist with such archaic thinking."

"Have you met Mr. Little?" she demanded.

"No, Gower is handling my business," he admitted.

"Then you better take a look at Little before you accuse me about my reactions. I swear his concept of morality comes straight from Victorian novels. He's the type to keep his nightclothes on when he makes love—once a month, providing his wife prods him!"

She stopped in embarrassment. Good Lord, what a crazy thing to pop out of her mouth! Kane threw his head back in a rich rumble of laughter that had the others on the terrace glancing at him with amusement. For the second time that day, the heat surged up to color her cheeks.

Still chuckling, he peered through the door. "I see Lydia steering them over to what's left of the buffet. Will you be all right here for a few minutes? I have to at least say hello to Tom. Then I'll give our regrets to the Bigelows. Do you think you can dredge up a headache or something so I can use it as an excuse for us to leave this soon?"

"Believe me, I don't have to invent one," she replied fervently. He started to the door and paused when he felt her hand on his arm. "I want to say thank you, Kane, for being so understanding."

Lights gleamed in the dark depths of his eyes as he took her hand and brought it to his mouth. "You'll find me very understanding if you give me half a chance."

Their eyes met and held for endless seconds before he turned away abruptly and left her. She watched his assured stride, unaware that her hand was pressed to her cheek.

"My salesmen get commissions for each new account they bring in," Kane commented as they pulled away in a cab. "I have a feeling I should put you on my payroll."

Once again he sat pressed too close, but Ellen refused to make an issue out of it by moving away. "Just recommend Foster Executive Services to your business friends when they come to New York, and I'll feel amply repaid," she said with forced lightness.

His scent should be outlawed for what it does to a woman, she thought in disgust. The closed-in cab seemed to be awash with it, making her feel dizzy. A glance from the corner of her eyes renewed her conviction of the stubbornness reflected in the square cut of his jaw. Her gaze shifted higher, giving her a view of the fascinating firmness in the wide slash of mouth. Was that control necessary to balance the passion hinted at by those clearly defined lips? Her gaze shifted resolutely to the photograph of the driver pinned to the windshield visor. *Stop it right now, Ellen Foster!* she warned forcibly.

The cab stopped by her apartment, and she simmered with irritation as Kane assisted her out before paying the driver. Her nerves were a mess and the sensation was disconcerting. Her plan was to say thank you in the lobby and escape. One thing she very definitely didn't want was Kane Windsor in her apartment. Not when her side was still burning from the heat of his body.

"I'll have a drink while we talk about tomorrow's itinerary," he said with calm assurance that left her gaping at him.

"The office has it already, and we can call you in the morning if there are any changes," she replied hopefully. The taxi sped down the street, and she wished she didn't abhor creating a scene. She should have insisted that he continue on in spite of the cab driver's knowing leer.

"But you already know there are changes," he stated firmly as he guided her with arrogant assurance up the three steps to the front entrance.

A sharp protest burned her mouth, only to be swallowed when Bernie came forward to hold open the

42

door. The guard's smile was so full of deference that it made her cringe. Recalling the outlandish tip that Kane had given the man earlier for getting a taxi so promptly, she knew he had turned his allegiance over to her enemy.

Not that she had the courage to start an argument in front of the doorman. But wait until they were in her apartment! She'd gone along with Kane's ploy because she owed him. But once they were finished discussing the suddenly important itinerary, he was going to find himself out the door so fast, he'd spin!

They went to the elevator, and his guiding fingertips were like rods of steel that transmitted his heat through her body. She sagged a little in defeat. Who was she trying to fool?

CHAPTER FOUR

"Coffee?" Ellen asked in a carefully controlled voice after the door to her apartment closed behind them. He was a client, after all, and had to be treated accordingly.

"A martini. I'll make it, if you don't mind."

Kane was already at the bar mixing the drink with practiced ease. Her eyes were stormy. He was taking over as if the place were his.

There was a wry smile on his firm lips as he handed the drink to her. "This takes less time. You have no need to be afraid of me and hide in the kitchen, Ellen."

She kept her gaze on the long fingers wrapped around the glass that he offered her. Had her irrational need to escape and regroup been that apparent? If so, she was in worse condition than she had realized! If she were this transparent in her business dealings, her dream would have never become a reality.

"I'm afraid I don't understand." *Liar!* Thank goodness she could avoid meeting his eyes. Hers remained fastened on the glass as she reached for it. The way he held it, made it impossible not to touch his fingers. The goblet was cool, with a faint film of condensation. Why, then, was heat coursing up her arm from the points of contact with his flesh?

The martini was perfect. Naturally! He didn't permit anything he did to be less than perfect, she conceded rashly. He stood at an arm's reach from her, and much too close again. The width of a room would be too close. She turned with an awkward movement and sank into a chair. No sofa for her, where he could join her and crowd her airspace!

"You said something about changes in your itinerary," she reminded him coolly after a refreshing sip of her drink. She watched as he chose the sofa and felt grim satisfaction that she'd been ahead of him on that maneuver.

His jet eyes glittered as they swept over her, then shifted to the bay window. "I must admit that your trees are growing on me." He paused to see her reaction to his unintentional pun. Her expression remained stoic, and he suppressed a sigh. She wasn't going to give an inch, which was all right with him. He was tired of women who made it all too easy. He thrived on challenges, which was why he had talked the home forces into buying an almost-defunct paper mill. No doubt that was also why this woman intrigued him with the fences she erected between them. "I think I'll try your idea for my home. My living room is large too. Maybe one of these trees would give it the lift it needs. What did you say its name was?"

"It's a Benjamii or weeping ficus, but there are many varieties. The well-known rubber plant is in the same family. I like this small-leaf type better because it makes a more subtle accent."

He nodded. "I'll give it a try and see how it survives our steam-heated winters." His gaze drifted around the room before fastening again on her. "I see evidence only of you here. Do you live alone in this big apartment?"

Ah, now game time begins. "If they can afford the rent, I believe most people prefer living alone." *Let him make of that what he can!*

45

"That can be lonely."

"Why don't you ask what you're trying to find out, Mr. Windsor? You want to know if there's a man in my life."

"It's Kane. Is there?"

"Many," she returned tartly. "I like most of the people I meet."

"But there is no one man?" he asked with a smile.

Her silver eyes grew stormy at his obvious satisfaction. "Since we're getting so personal, how is your love life? Is Miss Garcia waiting patiently for your return?"

His eyes narrowed a fraction. "Miss Garcia was my secretary."

Ellen gave an unladylike snort in derision. "I've had several appreciative employers, but none ever bought me a two-carat diamond pendant. Her typing skills must have been extraordinary."

His expression was iron hard. "I don't make a habit of explaining my actions to anyone, so consider yourself honored with this exception. Rita was the one and only time I ignored my policy not to mix business with pleasure. I soon realized it was a mistake, and it lasted all of two months. The diamond was a termination gift."

Ellen knew she was treading on dangerous ground, but an unusual excitement prodded her, driving her to taunt him further. "The thought is mind-boggling. I wonder what I could ask for if you should hire my services the next time you come to New York."

The feral smile was back. "Shall we try it and see?"

He leaned toward her, and she inhaled a cooling breath of air. Had the furniture actually shifted to bring him so close, smothering her with his sensuality? After bringing that Garcia woman into the conversation, she alone was to blame for the turn it had taken.

46

She couldn't fool herself any longer. The reason she was trying to stay away from this man was the blatant male sexuality that he exuded. It had destroyed her equilibrium at their first meeting, but she'd refused to accept the fact. Now her every instinct clamored with the warning that Kane Windsor was much too rich for her diet. Before she was tempted to taste, he had to be gotten out of her apartment.

"You forget that I'm hired by the investment house you're dealing with. And like you, my policy is never to mix business with pleasure," she returned primly.

His smile broadened. "Then you admit that getting to know each other better would be a pleasure."

Her glare was defiant. "I'm quite certain that you have the expertise to make knowing you a pleasurable experience. However, I'm not in the market for that particular experience, for several reasons. The most prominent is that I'm not interested." *Liar.* She was doing a lot of fabricating this evening.

Ellen was momentarily disconcerted when he drained his glass and rose. It wasn't that she was enjoying their exchange; she was simply riding a high and had been armed for his rebuttal. So she felt let down when he accepted her pronouncement without further argument. None of which made sense, she admitted. But had anything this evening?

"We still haven't discussed what changes you had in mind in your itinerary," she reminded him tartly as she accompanied him to the door.

"Just be ready at six tomorrow night when I come to pick you up."

"What?" She stared at him in disbelief. Hadn't he heard anything she had told him?

"That is, unless you'd rather eat after the show. Perhaps I could order a meal to be served in my suite."

47

"I don't believe what I'm hearing!" she cried sharply. "What you're saying is preposterous!"

"Is it?"

The terse rejoinder sent a shiver coursing down her back. Once again his finger curled under her chin, and as before, the hypnotic pull of his jet eyes made her unable to pull away.

"If I recall correctly, last year you accompanied us to a dinner, as well as on a shopping trip. I didn't hear any objections then, and I won't tolerate any now. Little and Gower *gave you* to me, and I intend to make full use of their generosity. It's agreed that neither of us intends to mix business with pleasure, so I don't see any reason for you to object."

How did he turn things around to make them sound so plausible? And why was it difficult to think clearly when she was close to him?

"Now answer me. Do you want to eat before or after the show?"

"Before," she whispered. No way was she going to his hotel suite again!

His smile showed satisfied pleasure. "There, that wasn't so difficult, was it?"

His head lowered slowly, and Ellen felt her mouth soften and part of its own volition. The last thing she saw before her lashes drifted to fan across her cheeks were the lights glittering in the darkness of his eyes.

The kiss was a faint brush of lips, a benevolent present for a lesson learned.

An intense hunger grew with startling force within her. The strength of her desire shocked her, and she pulled away with a twist to her head. Her one prayer was that he hadn't seen the intensity of her need or heard the smothered cry that tightened her throat at her denial.

She managed to open the door. "I hope your meeting tomorrow goes well." Her chin tilted in defiance, and she admitted to feeling a twisted sense of satisfaction when she glimpsed his frustration before he could hide it.

"Until tomorrow," he said.

A shiver coursed through her as she paused in turning the lock. Why did that sound like a threat—and a promise?

In spite of her doubt that it would come easily, sleep came a few short minutes after her head nestled on the pillow. It had been a difficult and strange day, and her emotional exhaustion put in its claim for rest.

It was midafternoon the following day, Tuesday, when frustration drove Ellen to throw down her pencil in disgust. Eyes that were the velvet black of a moonless sky insisted on coming between her and her reading material. Each rub of the coffee mug when she took a drink caused her lip to throb, reminding her how his touch had played havoc with her senses. Even more upsetting was how one fleeting kiss insisted on lingering like a brand.

He was a dangerous man. So why had she let him talk her into seeing him again that evening? Let him? He had assumed it was his God-given right that she comply willingly to his demand. Resentment, even anger, began to kindle deep within her. She fed it deliberately, using it to combat the undesired pull he exerted.

His arrogance was formidable, but she'd faced similar situations before and hadn't succumbed. What made this man so different that he was achieving such a tenacious hold on her thoughts? A cable from Arabia had arrived that morning from Abdul Hen-Sadik, a client she'd worked with before. He was arriving in three weeks with an entourage of thirty people. The logistics connected with their visit were staggering. She had no time for the intrusion of a Canadian who in twelve, no, eleven days would be gone.

Her concentration carried her through the worst of her workload. After much effort, she obtained a promise from the Plaza Hotel to place the Middle Eastern visitors in the same wing so they would have easy access to one another for better communication. She assigned Robin, one of her more promising assistants, to set up entertainment for the assorted wives. This called for diplomacy of the highest order. It would be a trial by fire. If Robin got through that assignment, she'd be able to handle anything.

By the time everything was arranged, Ellen was exhausted. Her only blessing was that Bella hadn't called, which, she hoped, meant that there were no problems with Kane and things there were under control. She groaned when she saw that it was after five. How in the world was she going to get home, shower, and be ready before he arrived at six?

At that hour, hunting for an empty taxi, of course, was an exercise in frustration. When she finally reached her apartment, her hand was trembling from tension, and she jammed the key forcefully in the lock. A fingernail snapped, and she slammed the door closed, leaving a trail of angry words as she hurried to the bedroom. Her glance took in the flashing red numbers on the digital clock on the bedside table: it was twenty minutes before Kane would be there.

Ellen was not one to linger over dressing, but this was cutting things a little too close. She kicked her shoes off as she applied an emery board to the ragged edges of her nail. She snatched clean underwear from a drawer with one hand as she tore her clothes off and flung them haphazardly onto her bed with the other. She was in the shower before recalling that she needed a new bar of soap. Water puddled on the carpet as she hunched down to get a fresh bar from the cabinet under the sink. As she turned to hop back into the shower, her shin made sharp contact with the open cabinet door.

Her words were decidedly blue as she hobbled back into the shower. A pink bruise expanded from the point of injury. There was no time to shampoo her hair. She winced when she gingerly soaped her leg. Her concentration was on easing the washcloth over the painful bruise when the spray hit her bent head. A screech of pure fury echoed in the tiled room, and Ellen shot out of the shower, searching in vain for a towel.

I don't believe it! This can't be happening! she seethed as she dripped all over the floor. She finally snatched towels from the side cupboard. A simple thing like preparing for an evening out couldn't have this many booby traps!

The clock flashed a new number, warning that five minutes were left. She used the hair dryer and struggled to apply makeup at the same time.

The dress was printed with fanciful green and blue blocks. It was casually elegant, with large dolman sleeves and a narrow skirt. It slid smoothly over her body, and she glanced at her reflection in the mirror with fleeting satisfaction as she fastened a heavy gold pin onto the dress's narrow collar. She couldn't have chosen a dress more different from the one she had worn the night before. This one covered her primly from neck to wrist, and the skirt had no seductive slit. She'd been lucky to discover shoes in matching green and blue, and she had to hunt through the closet to find even them.

Considering that nothing had gone right so far, she wasn't surprised that the shoes weren't in their accustomed place. Her temper, as well as her vocabulary, was getting a workout by the time she pushed through her clothes and found the errant shoes hiding in the far corner. Tension made her clumsy as she struggled to fasten the thin strap around her ankle. The doorbell chimed, and she glared at the clock in searing irritation. It was six o'clock exactly. Why couldn't the man have had the decency to be late?

And how had he gotten up here without Bernie's alerting her that he was on his way? That was an absurd question, she fumed, recalling how the doorman had practically genuflected before Kane the night before.

The bell pealed again. Clutching the sandal, she stomped angrily to answer it. Her shoe had a three-inch heel, and her awkward hobble impeded her progress. When the bell rang again, her temper went off like a skyrocket. Enough was enough! This man had given her nothing but aggravation since he arrived, and she had had it! Up to her neck!

The door was thrown open, and she glared at him, her silver eyes shooting poison darts. "My, what a busy finger you have!" she snarled.

A thick black brow rose in a sardonic arch. *What brought this on?* Kane wondered as he took in her flushed face and flashing eyes. His gaze swept over her, and he was amazed at the tightening of his body. This was how she would look after they had made love, with her usually carefully set hair in enticing disarray, her face flushed. Her breasts would heave in the same tantalizing way, but the cover they'd have then would be his hands, not some prim dress fastened securely high at her neck, a gold pin a guardian of untold riches.

He extended his arm to reveal a thin gold watch

52

fastened around his wrist. "It's six o'clock. This is the time agreed upon, isn't it?" he asked.

Ellen wasn't having any of that. He was all-too-devastatingly attractive in his dark blue silk suit, and the sight of him caused strange things to happen to her insides. He was suave and immaculate, and she was at a disadvantage knowing the mess her hair must be in after burrowing in the closet after the elusive shoes. The contrast between them was shattering, and her temper, already stretched to its limit, snapped.

"Oh, you're exactly on time," she seethed. "Why can't you be like the average person and come a little late?"

The eyebrow arched again. "Sounds to me like you were run a little ragged at the office."

His tone was all too explicit. *He* never allowed office pressure to become a hassle. If one couldn't stay on top of things, one had no business being the boss.

His condescending attitude was the last straw. "I happened to have a few problems that I doubt you can relate to," she snapped tartly. "A cable came this afternoon from a sheik in Saudi Arabia. He's bringing a party of thirty. Do you have any idea of the logistics involved? Try finding a first-class hotel willing to set aside that many rooms in one wing, far less on one floor! Do you have any idea what it's like riding herd on and entertaining the wives, not to mention—"

His head cocked in interest. "Wives, as in plural? How many does the poor man have?"

Her glare intensified. Her temper was seldom permitted to explode to this extent, and she was surprised by the primitive pleasure she was experiencing. "Who knows how many?" she snapped. "Why, do you want to see if it's worth changing your religion so you can indulge in some stupid polygamy?" She brandished

53

her shoe like a weapon. If he laughed at her, she'd let him have it!

"What has all that got to do with this balancing act on one foot?" he asked innocently.

That twitching in the corners of his lips better not turn into laughter! "That's why I'm running late!" she said through clenched teeth. "I was left with less than an hour to get home and dress. Naturally, the taxis ignored me. Then, because I was rushing, I broke a nail opening the damn door. I was so intent on racing the clock that I banged my leg on the cabinet when I found *after* getting wet in the shower that there was no soap. My hair got wet when I checked the bruise, and after finally drying it and getting it to look decent, it got all mussed up again when I had to hunt for these shoes. The stupid things were in the back of the closet."

She stopped abruptly in weary frustration, and her eyes closed to ease the sudden bite from threatening tears. Why was she carrying on like this? Kane, of all people, wasn't interested in the mess she managed to make of everything.

"Look," she offered tiredly, "why don't we just forget about this, and you go and enjoy your evening? In the mood I'm in, I'm the last one you want to be with. You'll find the tickets in your name at the box office."

He did smile then, but with tenderness that had her blinking. His arms extended, and the next thing she knew, one hand was pressing her head against his shoulder while the other gently patted her back.

"We all have our rough days," he murmured soothingly. "Suppose I fix us a drink so we can relax for a minute."

Ellen nodded, liking the feel of the silk jacket under her cheek. This secure feeling of having his strong arms around her was all too good. She inhaled deeply of his scent. Mixed with the warmth seeping through his suit, it drew the tension from her muscles until she collapsed gently against his solid body. For the first time in days—years—she felt at peace.

How long did the calm serenity last? One minute—five? Ellen didn't know. Gradually, a small but intrusive shift of awareness inserted itself. Her fingers resting on his upper arms were conscious of a growing tenseness to his muscles. Her breasts, pressed against his chest, registered a deeper breathing pattern that caused them to become hypersensitive in the confining bra.

Her head tilted back slowly, and their eyes met and held for long seconds. There was no thought of evasion. His kiss was a bare touch, a first languid assessment. When satisfied with the contours, the taste, his mouth molded over hers in a slow conformation. Thinking stopped immediately. The hunger that had overtaken her the evening before was at last being satisfied. This man, this joining of mouths, rapidly became her only existence. Sensations beyond any she had experienced before rippled in increasing waves, drowning her, until her legs forgot to support her and she sagged helplessly against his rock-hard body.

His hold on her mouth was released with obvious reluctance. "I think we better stop now," he said huskily.

"Why?" she cried rebelliously, raising her mouth for renewed possession.

"Because if we don't, we'll never make the show. I already missed out on one, and my sister is depending on me to tell her which are worth seeing when she comes here next month."

Ellen stared at him in disbelief. He removed her arms gently but firmly from around his neck, and she knew that whatever feelings had been aroused in him were under unbending control. If he could accomplish that minor miracle, so could she.

He pressed her gently into a nearby chair and bent to retrieve the sandal that had dropped from her grasp. Then, surprisingly, he knelt before her and raised her foot to rest on his knee.

"Ever since my nurse read 'Cinderella' to me, I always wanted to do this," he stated as he slipped the shoe onto her foot. "Of course, it's not a glass slipper, but I always thought they would be stiff to walk in and pretty uncomfortable."

Kane's grin was slightly lopsided, and Ellen had a sudden image of a small, dark-haired boy lost in childish fantasy while listening dreamily to fairy tales. "Ah, but you forget that the shoe had magic properties and adjusted to fit her." She watched in bemusement as he checked that the ankle strap was fastened correctly.

"Well, princess, this one seems to fit," he said with satisfaction. He glanced at her with a smile, and time seemed to be suspended as they stared at each other.

Ellen was vaguely aware of his hand gliding warmly up the calf of her leg. The sensations that the light touch produced had her catching her breath. His gaze dropped, and he stared as if in surprise at the position of his hand. He withdrew it as if he'd touched fire.

He cleared his throat and placed her foot carefully on the carpet before rising and going to the cabinet. His back was to her as he mixed a cocktail. She was thankful that he was performing that chore. Whatever special ingredient he mixed in his kisses made it impossible to recall which ones to use in the drink.

She watched the smooth ripple of muscles that his shoulders produced under the material of his jacket. The warning was loud and clear. One kiss, and she'd been ready to throw away her most stringent rule against fraternization with clients. Considering the unrequited ache deep within her, she was forced to confess with strict honesty that if he took her in his arms, she would deny him nothing.

Her head shook in bewilderment. She couldn't recall ever acting like this before. Nor had her reaction to a kiss ever been this extreme. It occurred to her that where Kane was concerned, all emotional responses were bigger than life. That fact made her decidedly uncomfortable.

This man was too potent and should be taken only in very small and careful doses. Her previous assessment returned with increased conviction. After tonight, future contact between them had to be made through the safety of her office.

CHAPTER FIVE

When they finished their drinks, Kane again consulted the thin gold watch nestled in the dark silken hair at his wrist. "I'm afraid we won't be able to have dinner before curtain time."

The delay was her fault, Ellen admitted. Earlier, after he had rejected her suggestion that he continue by himself, she'd returned to her room and perversely took her time getting ready to go. If only she could get rid of this tension!

Her stomach chose that moment to curl into a painful knot. Her hand pressed unconsciously to ease the ache, and he looked at her sharply. "If you're hungry, we can skip the play." A frown furrowed between his eyes. "You did that yesterday. Are you flirting with an ulcer?"

She looked at him, startled. That worry was repressed every time she reached for the bottle of antacids. If she remembered correctly, the discomfort had started when his name had first been given to her by Little and Gower. It had grown as each day brought his arrival closer.

"You've got to be kidding! I'm too young to have anything like that!" she returned sharply.

"Oh? And how young is too young? Children are known to develop them."

Ellen gasped in objection when he took her glass

from her hand. "If it's true, alcohol is the worse thing for you on an empty stomach," he said firmly, draining her drink. He marched to the kitchen, and she found herself trailing after him, sputtering in indignation.

"You need something to coat your stomach, like milk or cheese. It will ease the pain until we get to the restaurant. I bet you live on coffee most of the day."

Kane glanced at her over his shoulder after peering into the refrigerator. Catching her guilty nod, he glared at her. "Don't you have any common sense?"

He thrust a glass of milk into her hand, and Ellen was amazed to find herself drinking it docilely. She detested men who threw their weight around, yet a small previously unacknowledged part of her felt secretly pleased. It was nice to have someone care about her welfare for a change. She'd given him a hard enough time tonight, and maybe, for a while, she'd let him get away with acting bossy.

He cut a healthy chunk of cheese from a wedge of cheddar and placed it on a cracker. She nibbled on the offering while he cut another section for himself. How had she missed recognizing that there could be beauty in the graceful dexterity of a man's hands? The nails were pink with health and well maintained. The fingers were long and square cut, and the hint of black hair on them was downright sexy. Through some odd sixth sense, she recognized instinctively the strength and gentleness inherent in those hands, and she responded with a pulsing awareness.

Aghast at her own reaction, Ellen went to the sink to rinse her glass. She couldn't talk her way out of an evening with him, but one thing was certain: they had to leave now before he picked up on her feelings. To date, he'd shown remarkable sensitivity to her responses, and she couldn't, wouldn't, allow a repeat of that devastating kiss. That would tear her rule about fraternization to shreds. Also shredded would be the necessary contract from Little and Gower.

Nothing was worth having her dreams threatened, not even the bliss that she was certain would be hers in this Canadian's arms.

"I'm sorry I flew at you like a shrew," Ellen apologized as they drove away from her apartment.

Kane examined the pale oval of her face beside him. Did she have any idea how fascinating her silvery blue eyes were, or how intriguing her expression was when animated with high emotion? Was she really unaware that her agitation caused her breasts to push enticingly against the material of her dress, causing him to fantasize about how they'd feel cupped in his hands? Soft as silk, he was certain, and warm and responsive to his stroking.

"And I'm sorry that I inadvertently caused it." He captured her hand and held it reassuringly. "But I still hope you're smart and will make an appointment with a doctor."

He looked so concerned that Ellen couldn't make a production out of removing her hand. Besides, the soft rubbing he was performing felt inordinately soothing.

"There hasn't been time. Besides, I know what my problem is. When I'm under a lot of pressure, I forget to eat and end up drinking endless cups of coffee. When Bella's back, I'll tell her to remember to order sandwiches if I don't have time to go out. Bella loves to mother."

His firm lips softened into a wry smile. "I've noticed that tendency in her," he admitted.

The taxi stopped before La Cave Henri IV, a small French restaurant on East Fiftieth Street, and Ellen wondered what mothering Bella had dared to attempt on this dynamic and independent man. Fascinated by

60

the thought, she put it on her agenda to question her secretary the next time she called.

They ducked under the awning and descended the few steps into the cool dark interior. The maître d' greeted them in a charming French accent and led them to a table in a quiet corner.

"Will they serve us fast enough that we don't miss the beginning of the play?" she asked anxiously after the tuxedoed waiter handed them leather-backed menus.

"Forget about the play. We'll plan more carefully tomorrow evening and have a light snack before going to the theater."

Ellen gave an exasperated huff. What was the matter with the man? Didn't he hear a word she said? There wasn't to be a tomorrow.

He ignored her stormy glare. "Right now it's more important that you relax and eat."

If he could forget hundred-dollar tickets, that was fine with her. "Thank you for your care, Dr. Windsor. But what about the report to your sister?"

He looked at her obliquely. "I'll tell her she can read the reviews and make her own decisions. She always does anyway, through some convoluted process that no one understands."

Ellen liked the gentleness in his voice when speaking about his sister. It was obvious that theirs was a warm relationship. She felt a sudden desire to know more about this man who was invading too much of her time and thoughts.

"Your sister, is she married?"

His laugh held amusement. "Donna? I'd say very much so. She has three monsters to prove it."

"And you're a doting uncle."

He gave a wide, devastating smile. It lit up his eyes and caused tiny lines to fan out at the corners. "So

61

Jason, their father, accuses me. I tell him since he's so prolific, he should feel lucky that I enjoy prowling toy stores."

Ellen's face lit with interest. "Don't you go crazy over some of the toys they have now? My brother has a daughter who I just adore, but I keep urging him to try for a son so I can buy him trains. I always wanted a set of my own. When we were kids, Phil threatened to break my arm if I dared touch his. I had to wait until he was off playing with his friends."

Amused, he watched the impish smile spread on her face. "Did he ever catch you?"

"Once. My mother swears that when she heard the screams, she was positive we were being attacked. She bought me a toy stove as a consolation, but it wasn't what I wanted."

His hand was warm over hers. "I still have my set. When you come to Canada, I'll dig them out and let you play with them all you want. I should warn you, though, that they're quite extensive, and you'll need a week just to set them up."

There was something tender in his eyes that made Ellen grope for her glass of water. *No, no!* a small voice cried in defense. His mockery, even his passion, she could cope with, but not his tenderness. It let her senses wide open and vulnerable.

"Promises, promises," she dismissed lightly. "Do you have any plans to visit F.A.O. Schwarz?" she asked, naming the internationally famous toy store. The last time she was there, she had left sheepishly after spending an afternoon in unabashed fascination admiring the aisles laden with every imaginable toy.

"Of course. Why don't you come with me? It'll be a trade-off. Donna is expecting again. She states it's her last attempt for a daughter. You show me what little girls like, and I'll show you what's available should you ever get that nephew."

"With our luck, they'll have the same," Ellen predicted gloomily.

Kane squeezed her hand and laughed, then released it when the waiter arrived with the Boeuf en Daube that they'd ordered. She was dismayed at the way her hand wanted to creep across the table and return to the warm nesting place it had in his palm. This was a whole new set of responses that had nothing to do with what her rational mind defined as acceptable.

As the meal progressed, emotions, strong and evocative, gripped her. This very definitely had to be her last night with him. Her common sense was already threatening to flee under the force of his charismatic charm. It was foolish to deny the physical attraction growing between them. She was sliding further under his spell as they shared intimate memories.

They discovered that they both had strong, supportive parents who gave freely of their love yet cheered them when they had taken their initial flight from the nest. While Ellen had only her brother Philip, Kane was the eldest of four. The youngest and only girl was his sister Donna.

"Are your brothers married?" Ellen asked when the waiter removed their plates and divided the remaining wine in their glasses.

"Yes, and I've never taken the plunge, if that's what you're hinting for."

It was, and she was embarrassed that her interest was so obvious. "It's just that, being the eldest, it's logical to assume that you led them in 'taking the plunge,' as you call it."

"I thought of it a few times," he admitted. Catching her quick look of interest, he hid his smile. "The trouble was, the longer I thought about it, the less I could imagine being with that particular woman day after day. My attention span seems to be sadly lacking in some respects."

He did say Rita Garcia had lasted all of two months, she recalled. That should tell her something, but why in the world should that matter to her? In little more than a week, he'd be safely back in Canada. She could then get her life back in order, thank goodness.

After the exchange of family stories, Ellen felt free to ask him something she had been wondering about since she'd first met him. "Do you have any Indian ancestors?" she questioned. She wasn't prepared for the guarded look that came to his eyes.

"I do," he admitted after taking a sip of wine. "My great-grandfather was an English trapper, and he married what I hear was a beautiful woman from the Muskekowug tribe. That's a branch of the Eastern Cree Nation. Does that bother you?"

The question sounded harsh, and she looked at him in surprise. "I don't see any reason why it should. I was wondering about it because of your black hair." And those dark, all-seeing eyes, and those fascinating slanting cheekbones, she added silently.

Her explanation seemed to satisfy him. A melt-in-the-mouth chocolate mousse was served for dessert, and only then did Ellen realize that the meal was almost over. They had talked of many subjects, yet she felt as if they could continue for days and barely touch all the ones they had mutual interest in. Not that they agreed on everything, but they seemed to respect each other's positions.

Why had fate made this man who interested her on every level a client and thereby placed him off limits? She sighed in regret as they walked to the corner to hail a cruising taxi.

"Are you feeling better?" Kane asked a few minutes

later. "You haven't rubbed your stomach since you ate."

Had he been that concerned? "I enjoy eating when food is placed before me, otherwise I seem to forget about it," she admitted.

He shook his head in exasperation. "You need a keeper, Ellen. The human body is a wonderful machine, but it needs fuel to work. Neglect it, and you'll soon find yourself in trouble."

"Yes, Dr. Windsor."

He frowned at her sternly. "Why do I have the feeling that that bit of advice went in one ear and out the other?"

She blinked with wide innocent eyes. "But I remember every word you've spoken." That was all too true, she realized in surprise.

Kane wondered why he was so concerned. One would think her welfare was important to him. And it was, he realized with a start, as he gazed into her teasing silvery eyes. In a sudden need to banish further thought, he bent swiftly over her, forcing her back against the seat.

"How about a little respect?" he warned. Before she could object, his mouth settled over hers. *At last,* something deep within him sighed, and he knew that this was what he'd been hungering for ever since waking up that morning with this tantalizing woman on his mind.

He felt as if her lips were made for his. No mouth ever conformed so perfectly to his so that together they made a whole. The thought disturbed him, but she trembled and softened under his hands, causing a fire to spark and leap through his veins.

A silken strand of hair tangled around his finger, and he remembered how enticingly disheveled it had been. How he would love to see the whole glorious

65

mass spread over a pillow. His pillow. His hand followed the slope of her shoulder, the smooth line of her rib cage, the curve of her waist, and the feminine swell of her hip. He recalled how her leg felt when he had fastened her shoe.

He wanted this woman with a demanding need, and he was certain from her responses that the feeling was mutual. What an unexpected, delightful bonus she was to his trip!

He released her mouth, and a tiny sound passed her kiss-swollen lips in objection. He gazed with satisfaction at her flushed face, the passion glittering darkly in her remarkable eyes. "It's years since I've done any necking in the backseat of a car," he murmured with a wry shake of his head. "Shall we continue this in the comfort of your apartment?"

Assured of her compliance, Kane had meant it as a rhetorical question, so he was unprepared for her reaction. Ellen stared at him blankly as if returning from a distant land. She seemed not to understand what was implied. Her hands, which seconds before had been curled tenaciously around his neck, slid against the hard wall of his chest and pushed.

Once free, she pressed against the far side of the cab. The flush of passion was replaced with the heat of anger. "I believe you must have a hearing problem. I told you this is my last evening with you, and it most definitely isn't going to end in bed. I'm certain that you're an expert lover, but please save your seduction scenes for someone who'll appreciate them more."

The taxi jerked to a halt before her apartment. His kisses had wrought their usual havoc, and she reached blindly for the door handle to escape.

His hand closed over hers, stilling its groping. "A simple no would have sufficed," he told her coolly. "I'll be here tomorrow at the same time."

She glared at him in anger. What did she have to do to get her message through his thick skull that there would be no tomorrow? "I'm sorry, but I have a previous date."

"Cancel it!"

Their eyes clashed. His held a cool assurance that his order would be obeyed. Hers sparkled with righteous anger,

"I'll make believe I didn't hear that," she said icily. "Now, if you please, I've had a long, tiring day and need my sleep."

He released his hold on the handle. Why was he permitting her to get to him like this?

He watched sourly as she walked with stiff dignity, until the entrance door closed behind her. "Damn!" he muttered after giving his address to the smirking driver and settling back into the seat. He could read the man's mind as if he'd spoken aloud. *So you didn't score, buddy. So what? I can take you to someone who'll be happy to take care of your problem. For a price.*

Kane had the addresses of several women he could call. And they wouldn't hide behind a hackneyed excuse like nonfraternization, or send him away in the condition he was in.

But none had auburn hair that caught fire when touched by the sun, or silver blue eyes that could laugh and tease and darken seductively with passion, or had lips that beckoned even as they guarded a mouth that held the nectar of the gods.

He stared without seeing at the passing scene as the taxi stopped and started in the endless traffic. It looked as if there were two courses open for him to take as far as Ellen Foster was concerned. He could bow to her wishes and not see her again, or he could accept the challenge and storm the bastion she was hiding behind.

A hard smile formed. The second option certainly held much more appeal. As he'd told her, his family knew that he loved and accepted all challenges. He saluted her in a silent toast. She had her warning. May the best contestant win! His smile became complacent. Kane had no doubt who the winner would be.

CHAPTER SIX

The first thing Ellen did when she arrived at her office the next day was to call Bob Stemler. Considering Kane's track record, she had half-expected him to follow her the night before and press his demand that she cancel her date. He was arrogant enough to assume she'd bow to his order, and she was wary enough to guess that he wasn't finished with his pursuit. She remembered all too clearly his assertion that he thrived on challenges. She had an uncomfortable feeling that he considered her a challenge and was arming for combat. She might be wise to reinforce her defenses. He'd shown an alarming talent for knocking them down.

"Hello, counselor," she greeted cheerfully when Bob's secretary put her through. "It occurred to me that I haven't seen you for a while and thought I'd touch base."

"Why, hello, angel," he responded. "What is it, two, three months? Blame it on the workload."

Ellen felt her tension dissolve as she relaxed in her chair, and a smile touched her lips. She and Bob had met at a cocktail party shortly after she started Foster Executive Services. They began as friends, drifted into a short affair, and decided that they preferred being friends, without the sexual hassle. Lovers were easy enough to come by; a good friend was far more difficult to find.

"Considering the hungry mouths depending upon you for food, it's a good thing the clients keep coming," she teased. Bob's hobby was breeding Thoroughbreds. He sold them to be trained elsewhere, and when one of the horses he had bred won the Preakness, they had celebrated with champagne at Sardi's. "And talking about hungry mouths, can I interest you in dinner tonight so you can tell me about all your conquests on and off the track—and courthouse?"

"You lucky girl. I happen to be without a date and am free to accommodate you," he agreed with a laugh.

"You're all heart," she returned drily. "See you at seven?" She wasn't about to get herself caught in a last-minute rush two nights in a row.

She replaced the phone with satisfaction. *That* loose end was taken care of. Now her defense was solid in case Kane should try to sweet-talk her into succumbing to his will. A faint frown creased her brow. Did she really have so little resistance where he was concerned? Remembering how she melted under his heated kisses, she reluctantly had to admit that she didn't.

Robin brought in the list of the women in the Saudi Arabian party. Drawing on her years of experience as a protocol officer, Ellen saw at a glance that only three were of high enough rank to demand their specialized services. One was Abdul's wife and the other two were married to his two top assistants. The rest were married to lesser officers. For them, she ordered a list of available entertainment and of specialty stores dealing in high-quality but not overly expensive merchandise. She could always rely on Bloomingdale's for these people. They had little in common with the ranking three, and from experience she knew they'd be more at ease going their own way. Someone else from her staff would be assigned to attend to their needs.

She was involved with Robin in setting up the necessary entertainment when her phone rang. She answered with an absent hello and was unprepared for the heat that shot through her veins when she heard Kane's deep voice.

"Hello, princess. Did you eat a good breakfast this morning?"

Ellen glanced guiltily at the cup of coffee cooling on her desk. "Well, I was a little rushed," she admitted lamely. She'd tossed in bed until the early hours because of this disturbing man, and sleep had come late, but that piece of information was hers alone.

He breathed an exasperated sigh into her ear. "And you haven't had time for anything but coffee," he hazarded with assurance.

That and several antacids, she admitted silently.

"I guessed right, didn't I?" he chastised. "And I bet you haven't made an appointment with your doctor."

"I have one set of parents, Kane," she warned. "I don't need any more."

He ignored her reprimand. "Things should be cleared here by twelve. I'll be there and take you to lunch."

Ellen's heels dug into the carpet as if she were applying a brake. Oh, no he wasn't! She'd had all a person could take of one Kane Windsor without becoming a casualty. "Thank you, but that's impossible," she stated firmly. "I'm swamped with work and simply don't have the time,"

"I suppose you'll order a sandwich and expect that to be adequate."

"Correct the first time." If she remembered.

"Well, if you can't make lunch, I'll see you tonight

and make certain you have at least one decent meal in you!"

"I already told you that I have a date." Thank you, Bob, for coming through, she blessed silently.

"You can be the most exasperating—!" Kane sucked in his breath in annoyance. "I'll be in touch," he said, and slammed the receiver down. Why was he letting this ungrateful wretch get to him? Let her get an ulcer! He wouldn't be around to see her suffer!

Bella entered the conference room with the folder he'd requested.

Kane placed the folder on the table and leaned back to study the woman. He demanded perfection from the people who worked for him, and he knew he wasn't the easiest person to work for. He admired Bella's easy sense of humor, which never seemed to ruffle under pressure. Except for the fact that he knew she'd never leave her home and family, he wouldn't be above trying to lure her away from Ellen. He could offer a higher salary, but he suspected that that wouldn't be enough to shake Bella's loyalty to her present boss.

"I was just speaking to Ms. Foster," he said casually. "I was trying to set up a lunch so we could go over some business, but she couldn't make it."

Bella gave a motherly cluck. "I wish you had succeeded. That woman is her own worst enemy. I'm always after her about working so hard and not eating right. Sometimes I think she runs on nerves alone. And those endless cups of coffee."

His black brows lowered in consternation. "Couldn't you see that she at least had something?"

Her shoulders lifted in resignation. "I've given up counting how many half-eaten sandwiches I've thrown out. She gets so involved that she forgets that they're there."

"Mr. Gower tells me they're planning to sign a contract with your company. Surely she makes enough to pay for an adequate staff to take on some of the work-load!"

"It isn't quite like that," Bella explained, not realizing that Kane's questions were causing her to reveal the problems and worries that were plaguing her boss. True, Ellen was foolish to have locked herself prematurely into her expansion and tie up her cash flow, especially since she was still on trial with Little and Gower. But she was a hard worker, and everyone on her staff was rooting for her success.

Bella sat down and prepared to take notes. She was unaware of the thoughtful expression on Kane's face.

Ellen dropped her pencil and arched her back to ease the muscles that were tired from bending over the desk. "I guess that's as much as we can do until we get more information from Abdul's office."

Robin gathered the sheets of notes and slipped them into a folder. "I'll see about those blocks of theater tickets after lunch," she promised. She glanced at the weary face across from her. "You look like you could stand a break from all this. I found this fabulous little ma-pa restaurant just two blocks away. How about joining me and defy all with a calorie-laden fettucini?"

Ellen looked at the two reports that were already late in going out and smiled her regrets. "Another time," she promised. "I'll have Sue call out for a sandwich." The light on her intercom blinked, and she pressed the button.

"There's a—oh, dear, sir, you can't go in unannounced!" Ellen heard Sue's voice hesitate in confusion. The door swung open, and Ellen looked up questioningly.

"Kane!" His name was a whisper of surprise and

pure undiluted joy. She had thought herself purged of the unsettling effect he could produce, but that had been an illusion.

He walked in, and immediately the room was his. Everything diminished in contrast to his vibrancy. She had a quick glimpse of Robin's stunned expression before her attention fastened on the two men following him, carrying a large tray between them. Sue stood behind them, her hands fluttering in apprehension. She'd been overwhelmed by her new responsibilities since Bella had left, and nothing had prepared her for how to cope with this.

"I'm s-sorry, Ellen," she stuttered helplessly.

"It's all right," Ellen managed to say. "You can go back to finish that letter."

"You said you couldn't take time off for lunch, so I brought it here," Kane stated. "I had the hotel prepare something for us. I'm sure you'll love it."

He waved a hand at the space in between the two chairs across from her desk, and the men snapped open the attached legs and set the tray, now a table, carefully on the floor. The cloth was whipped off the domed cover, revealing a service for two. Chilled asparagus soup was poured from a Thermos. Seeing a delicious seafood salad nestling in crisp greens, Ellen suddenly realized how hungry she was. Bills passed hands, and Kane told the men they'd be notified when to return for the tray.

Robin gazed with amusement at her boss, who for once seemed to be at a loss, and then at the tall dark man, before glancing at the tempting food. "Some sandwich!" she murmured slyly with a grin before slipping from the room.

"Ready to eat, princess?" Kane asked as he held the chair for her. The revealing flash of joy that she hadn't been able to hide had been worth the pressure he had

had to apply to accomplish this feat. The little minx wasn't as immune to him as she pretended to be. But he didn't fool himself that he was home free yet. There were still a lot of bricks in that wall to be knocked down. And after what seeing her again was doing to him, he was going to get a lot of enjoyment out of tearing the rest away one by one.

"You must be absolutely crazy," Ellen said helplessly. What kind of defense could a woman build against a man who did charming things like this?

"Not crazy, princess, just hungry."

Ellen busied her hands with adjusting the napkin so that he wouldn't notice their trembling. His slumbering look showed to which hunger he was referring. It was too much like the one that had kept recurring in her dreams the night before, resulting in her awaking to twisted sheets in the morning.

She tore away from her thoughts. With stern resolution, she selected a spoon and tasted the chilled soup. "Delicious. And perfect on a hot day," she murmured primly.

He smiled. He'd have to remember to watch those expressive eyes. Except for that initial unguarded second, she was good at camouflaging her emotions.

"Are your June days usually this hot?" he asked conversationally. "I called home this morning, and they're still wearing light coats."

"June can be anything, though today is exceptionally warm. If the weekend is like this, I can imagine the rush to the beaches," she admitted. He unwrapped the napkin on the bread dish and offered her a still-warm croissant.

She speared a plump shrimp and looked at him with questioning amazement. "I just realized—how did you know these are my favorites?"

75

"Bella!" they said in unison. "She's as concerned about your eating habits as I am," Kane stated.

"Bella enjoys mothering a little too much," Ellen said.

His eyes laughed at her. "I hope you don't think I'm into being paternal!"

She swallowed a tender section of lobster before answering. "I doubt there's a woman alive who would think of you along those lines," she said tartly.

"Good. I'm glad to see you have the proper focus. What time shall I come for you tonight?"

She glared at him in exasperation. "This is beginning to sound like a broken record. I *do* have a previous engagement, if you recall. Even if I didn't, I'd have no intention of seeing you tonight, tomorrow night, or any other one as long as you are here. Is that finally understood?"

His smile was consoling. "It isn't good for the digestion to get worked up while you're eating, princess," he soothed. "Try one of these muffins while they're still warm."

The muffins *were* tempting—to use as missiles. It took a major effort not to use them as such. Several deep breaths were necessary to divert Ellen's attention back to the salad. It was delicious, and she should know better than to let him get such a rise out of her. Unfortunately, where he was concerned, her emotions were all too volatile, and he seemed to enjoy treating them as a tinderbox.

"How is Ms. Agee?" she asked stiffly, switching abruptly to the first subject that came to mind. "When I call the hospital, all they tell me is that she's doing as well as can be expected."

"She was moved to a private room late yesterday. I stopped by earlier to see her. She's over the worst of the experience. They're talking about releasing her tomorrow, and I plan to send her home to recuperate. These attacks can take a lot out of a person."

Ellen heard the care in his voice and wondered just how immune he was to his secretary. If his libido were so difficult to contain that he once slipped with the sultry Rita Garcia, what was to prevent him from succumbing again? From Jeanne's report, the new secretary had a delicate beauty. The change from her predecessor in itself might be a lure.

She shifted in her chair to ease the uncomfortable feeling curling tightly within her. "Then I better make the time to see her this afternoon. I feel terrible that we were responsible for sending her to the hospital— even though it was a mistake."

He stared at her. What was going on in her mind, causing this withdrawal? "Frances will enjoy it. She doesn't know anyone in New York, and she's pretty lonely."

Ellen poked through the lettuce leaves for an elusive piece of crabmeat. "I meant to ask you before, was your meeting with Miles Walker successful?"

"Looking for your commission?" he teased gently. "Yes, I think we can come to terms. I'm sending one of my salesmen to work out exactly what his requirements are and how we can best help him."

By the time they were finished eating, Kane was having trouble containing his frustration. On the surface, their conversation was relaxed and sharing, but whenever he pressed for more intimacy, he came up against that wall. He'd made points with this lunch, but she wasn't letting his pursuit get beyond that, and he didn't have time right now to push for more.

He extended his arm to check his watch. "Will you have your secretary call the hotel and tell them that we're finished so they can pick up the tray?" he asked

77

after setting the dome in place. "I'm afraid I have to go now, or I'll be late for my next appointment."

"It's the least I can do," Ellen said as she walked him to the door. Thank goodness he was finally leaving—a few minutes more of his unsettling presence and all her resolutions would have flown out the window. She was already regretting her panic call to Bob. Surely, just because Gower had turned up at the party two nights ago didn't mean she could see him again. The fact loomed large in her mind that there were only eight days left before Kane was gone and she'd perhaps never see him again.

She drew in a steadying breath. This was madness! All he had to do was be in the same room with her, and her objectivity crumbled. They paused by the door, and she put her best smile in place. Knowing all too well what meeting his eyes could do to her stability, she didn't dare look at his face. Instead, she stared at the silk burgundy tie fastened under his strong chin.

"Have I thanked you for lunch?" she asked. "It was a lovely gesture." *Go now, please, before I take that fatal step closer.* Something alien in her was pushing to feel the strength of his arms around her one last time, to revel again in the glory his kisses could arouse in her.

"You'd find me full of lovely gestures if you'd give me the opportunity." Dammit, he hadn't gone through all this just to receive a polite smile! Why didn't she look at him, so he could bathe in the silver in her eyes? And that succulent mouth, he wanted to feel it soften and tremble under his—he stopped short with a sharp inhalation. It *was* trembling!

"Ellen!" The groan whispered from deep within him. There was no way that he could stop his hands from reaching for her. There was no way he could stop them from curling around her neck, from sliding down the gentle arch of her back and cupping the delicious

78

curve of her buttocks and anchoring her to him. And there was absolutely nothing that could stop his mouth from closing over hers and making it his.

He'd never felt hunger like this, he realized with shattering amazement. Her mouth tasted of the strawberries in champagne that they'd had for dessert, and more. The soft flesh at her neck felt like warm silk. Her body melting against his spoke of surrender. He'd had his full share of women, but he knew at some subliminal level that this special person was all women, and very much more.

Why that conviction held truth was beyond his understanding. He was lost in her perfume. It reminded him of lazy summer days and the scent of crushed wildflowers. He tasted all the nuances of flavors hidden in her mouth and drew them deep within him, where they were his to savor forever.

His hands molded and caressed each curve, committing them to memory. When the fullness of her breast rested in his palm, he knew he needed more. Her clothes became an obscenity, hiding her from him. He had to eliminate them. Now.

He raised his head to search for the closure, and only then did rational thought return. They were in her office. He was so lost in his arousal that he had been ready to take her on the floor. Never had he been this out of control, and the realization of where his passion had almost taken him was a further shock.

He had to clear his throat twice before he could speak. "I—we—that was pretty spectacular, princess." She even had him stuttering like a blasted adolescent! "I knew I shouldn't have booked this appointment, but I'm afraid I'd better hurry. Take care."

He brushed a chaste kiss onto her cheek. Chaste! After what they'd just experienced, where did he dredge that up from?

Later, Kane had only a dim recollection of leaving her office, of going down the elevator. He walked three blocks before coming to his senses enough to flag down a taxi. Even then, the picture of her eyes, wide and dazed from the effect of that kiss, remained imprinted, and he had the uncomfortable feeling his had looked the same.

CHAPTER SEVEN

Ellen shifted the ceramic bowl that held baby pink rosebuds to her other hand and peered into the open doorway. Frances Agee, she saw, did have the delicate beauty that Jeanne had described. Her ash-blond hair was drawn back from her fine-boned features with an orchid ribbon that matched the ruffled bed jacket she wore.

Frances caught the movement by the door. An eyebrow arched delicately in question at the newcomer as a tentative smile of greeting parted her lips.

"I'm Ellen Foster from Foster Executive Services, Ms. Agee," Ellen explained as she offered the bowl of roses. She could imagine how Jeanne must have felt when first meeting her. Those flaming scarlet roses that had been ordered for her arrival were definitely the worst possible choice they could have made. "Mr. Windsor told me that you could have visitors, and I had to come to offer my apologies for what happened."

Frances's slender fingers caressed a velvet bud before she looked up with a rueful grimace. "I admit I had some awful thoughts when the allergic reaction began building. Since then, Mr. Windsor has explained that the chef was to blame for the shrimp stock and that you were entirely innocent."

Ellen sighed as the nagging worry over a possible

81

lawsuit finally disappeared. "Believe me, if I had known about your allergy, I would have made certain that the kitchen knew about it too. If you're doing much traveling with Mr. Windsor, it might be a good idea to see that the information goes ahead of you."

"I don't think that will be necessary. My husband doesn't like me traveling without him in the first place, and after this episode, he's put his foot down." Her face grew wistful. "I hope that won't cost me my job. Mr. Windsor is a great employer and the work is challenging, but I was hired with the understanding that there were times I'd have to go on trips like this one."

There was no reason for Ellen to feel a rush of relief when she heard that this attractive woman was married. Hadn't she just gone through chaos during the hour since Kane's departure? It had been impossible to concentrate because her blood kept reheating with each recollection of his kiss. In desperation, she had fled the office still haunted by him and came to visit his secretary. It had been a poor choice. She had no desire to hear Frances Agee extol Kane Windsor. Now that it was evident that there was nothing between the two, it removed the hope that she could fault him for using her as a substitute.

But, feeling better, Frances had been bored with her enforced inactivity and now frankly welcomed her visitor. "When I heard about your company, I was very interested. Tell me, how did you get a business like that going? If I get fired, I might consider starting one in Toronto."

Ellen had no difficulty talking about her pet subject, and she explained some of the basic problems that had to be overcome first. "And now I guess I have expansion fever. I'm planning two more offices," she concluded with satisfaction. "People in other cities have contacted me, and I'm toying with the idea of setting up more franchises. My main concern is maintaining control. I don't have to tell you how the concept can be misused. My greatest problem is locating managers that I can trust to keep the company's reputation unblemished."

Ellen frowned. *My, I'm being pontifical.* Two hours ago she had been panting in a mutual seduction with her client. If Kanc hadn't managed to dredge up control, they'd have been making wild and delicious love on the carpet. That it would have been earthshaking, she had no doubt. She was strong willed and no fool. Time was needed to diminish the chemistry between them. Until that was accomplished, distance was important.

"If you're really interested, I should warn you that a lot of market research has to be done first," Ellen continued. "Hotels have to be visited to check for quality and service. Restaurants need investigating, not only for the menu options but the standards of the chef. Many clients prefer ethnic foods, so you have to find someone who understands the cuisines of many countries and can rate them. Then there's entertainment. Every type has to be unearthed and filed for quick reference, and even more important than that are the stores. You'll find that the women, especially, love to spend money shopping, so every specialty shop has to be catalogued. The problem I found the most difficult was finding banks that would honor foreign checks for quick money, and I mean in the thousands."

Frances gaped in awe. "I had no idea all that was involved!"

Ellen smiled grimly, remembering the year of endless work she had struggled through before signing her first contract. And it never ended; the vital files needed constant updating.

"Only when you have that information at your fingertips can you begin the really difficult part—convincing investment houses and companies who cater to out-of-state or foreign clients that they need your services. Windsor Enterprises should be a good place to begin. You should be able to pick up some business on the contacts you've made through them."

The pale face was alight with interest. "My husband is a super salesman. I can get pointers from him. I also have a friend who is a fashion buyer. She's been my source when I'm looking for something out of the ordinary. She'd love to help."

Ellen left, amused by the woman's enthusiasm. Maybe setting up franchises was the way to go. A cadre of investigators could be sent to a prospective city. They'd do the time-consuming and frequently frustrating preliminary work. It would be part of the package deal. The concept intrigued her and occupied her mind, so she could finally forget about Kane Windsor for a little while.

But it didn't work that evening. Although Bob Stemler's hair was dark, it wasn't midnight black; neither did it have the vibrancy her fingers encountered when they were buried in Kane's hair. She knew his tan was from careful nurturing under lamps at the Athletic Club; it seemed pallid in comparison with the healthy color that Kane sported, the result, he'd told her, of a recent fishing trip into the hinterlands of Canada.

When he came for her, Bob had looked at her with appreciative speculation that she couldn't miss. Ellen wondered if he was picking up on lingering remnants of the passion she'd experienced that afternoon. All through the meal, he practiced a subtle seduction, and she wished that there were a response she could dredge up in return. The thought flitted through her

84

mind that perhaps one passion could be used to erase another, but it faded quickly. Bob was a friend. She couldn't use him that way, although she was certain he'd be only too happy to go along with her experiment. She sighed in reluctant acceptance. Bob would never do. He was the wrong man.

The next morning, Thursday, Jeanne tried to hide her dismay when Ellen informed her that Kane Windsor was her case again.

"Are you certain you want me to? After that first introduction, I have the feeling I'm not one of his favorite people."

"There's no reason you can't keep a low profile. He's settled in, and all you need to do is check with him every day to see if there are any changes. Just make certain that he gets the tickets each night for the shows he wants to attend." Ellen had no doubt that by now Kane must have found someone to accompany him. Her hand pressed her middle to ease the sudden ache, and she looked sourly at the cup on her desk. She'd rushed out that morning without breakfast, and she'd lost count of the number of cups of coffee she'd already had. Maybe Kane was right and she needed to develop more sensible eating habits.

An hour later, Jeanne was back, pleading. "Look, I'll help you all you want and even work overtime on my own on the case from Saudi Arabia, only take back Kane Windsor! Please, just please, don't ask me to have anything more to do with that impossible man!"

Ellen leaned back in the chair and slipped her hands to her lap where they clenched. "Now what did he do to you?" she asked with a sigh.

"He didn't *do* anything. It's just that I'm too young to die from frostbite."

"How did he look?" Oh, God! Jeanne must think

85

she'd flipped her lid. And she wouldn't be far wrong. Ever since Ellen awoke that morning, she had tried to eliminate thoughts of the Canadian awaking with some beauty beside him, of slender hands that weren't hers indulging in the delightful adventure of rubbing through the hair on his chest. If Jeanne reported that he looked tired and sated, she didn't know what she'd do. Scream, at least.

Jeanne stared at her blankly. "I wouldn't know. I spoke to him over the phone. It was a direct conduit to an icehouse. I don't know what's bugging him, but the impression was loud and clear that he's not pleased that you aren't in charge. You must admit that I've been faithful and true and have stayed with you through all emergencies," she begged piteously, "but there's a limit to what a poor human can take. I don't know how I could have been misled so easily. I thought I was being given the keys to heaven when you first assigned that hunk to me." She shook her head sadly at the blow that fate had dealt her.

Ellen smiled appreciatively at Jeanne's theatrics. Having been another recipient of Kane's arctic blasts, she could sympathize with her. But there was no way she was going to change the status quo. "You have my condolences, but I have faith that you'll survive. Just think of this as an opportunity to strengthen your character."

"And you look too lovely to be so heartless," Jeanne said. Her attention wavered as she stepped aside to let Sue bring in the mail. "My, what did you buy at F.A.O. Schwarz?" she asked, peering at the package Sue placed on her desk. "Is it something for your niece?"

"I haven't been near the store for months," Ellen said. She picked up the package and shook it carefully. "Maybe it's a condolence for all the money I've dropped there."

"Well, open it," Jeanne urged, handing her the letter opener. "I'm the kind that can never keep a present until Christmas."

"You mean you're the nosy type," Ellen teased. The tape parted under her prying, and she slapped her friend's hands away as she pulled back the cardboard flaps.

"Oh!" Ellen felt the blood drain from her face as she lifted out the toy. It was oval, with villages and forests lithographed on the metal surface. She pressed the lever, and a tiny train whirred around the track, which was bent in a figure eight. It gave an equally tiny toot as it disappeared into the tunnel going through a mountain raised on one side.

"How perfectly adorable!" Sue gushed.

Jeanne looked questioningly at the stunned face of her boss as she handed her the small envelope that was at the bottom of the box. "It's not what you usually pick for your niece."

"No, it isn't, is it," Ellen admitted dazedly. She read the message on the card and, after a heartbeat, dropped it silently into her drawer.

"Come on, Sue, back to the salt mines," Jeanne said, taking the typist's arm and hurrying her from the room. She had no idea what that was all about, but it didn't take much to see that her boss needed to be alone. She looked like she didn't know whether to laugh or cry.

When the door closed, Ellen slowly retrieved the card, not that she needed it to know what it said. *At last! Your very own set of trains. The invitation is still open to play with mine.* A heavy *K* was scrawled as a signature.

Oh, Kane, what are you doing to me? she thought. The train gave a faint toot and slowly wound down.

He must have bought it before she had locked the door between them, before that earthquake of a kiss

87

that was still sending waves of aftershock through her. She sucked in a wavering breath. If he called now, she knew it would be beyond her power to resist him.

Her chin firmed, and she punched a button on her intercom. "Sue, make certain all calls from Mr. Kane Windsor go to Jeanne even if he asks for me. Is that understood?"

"Sure, Ellen." Curiosity was evident in Sue's voice. Ellen grimaced, knowing her request would be more grist for the office-gossip mill, which was already churning after the impromptu lunch Kane had shared in her office.

She forced her attention to the rest of the mail Sue had brought in. It was mostly bills associated with the two offices awaiting their grand openings. She was past the point of no return with them, and she knew that the money drain had to stop soon. The contract with Little and Gower was a stark necessity.

"Mr. Windsor called twice," Sue notified here when she came in later with letters for her signature. "He wanted to speak with you and was very unhappy when I told him he had to speak to Jeanne instead."

Ellen's hand wavered only a microinch before steadying. "Jeanne hasn't come in with a seared ear, so I guess she was able to handle his requests."

"Oh, he hung up before I could connect him." *Slammed the phone down, was what he really did,* Sue thought, but she decided not to tell her boss the whole truth upon seeing her grim expression.

It's seven, going on six days, Ellen reassured herself doggedly. Surely she could resist any pressure he might exert on her for the remaining time that he was here!

That afternoon she wasn't so sure, when Sue notified her that Tom Gower was on the line. *This is it* was her first resigned thought as her remaining options did a frantic dance in her head. Before scrapping her dream, she'd cut her salary in half and pare her expenses to the bone. Drawing in several calming breaths, she told Sue to put him through.

"How are you, my dear? I'm just checking in with you about the Windsor case you're handling for us."

Ellen hated to be called "my dear," especially in the unctuous tone that Gower used. If Kane had finally dumped the fiasco of that first day onto his lap, she preferred Gower to come straight out about firing her. "I hope everything is meeting with your approval," she replied briskly.

"I must say you handled the unhappy episode concerning his secretary's illness with remarkable adeptness. It was quick thinking, sending your secretary in to fill in. I'm seriously considering luring Mrs. Carstairs away from you, so don't be surprised when it happens. She's exceptional."

His *heh, heh* was a weak excuse for a laugh, and Ellen gritted her teeth. "She is also extremely loyal, or I wouldn't have risked letting her go to help Mr. Windsor," she said, keeping her tone light. Was he getting his kicks by drawing out the suspense before letting the ax fall?

"Ah, yes, our client, Mr. Windsor. Which brings me to the reason for this call. As you know, we are an investment firm. Our primary function is to invest our clients' money so they accrue the most profit. It is all built on a tenuous thing called trust, and to build that trust, we need to have their undivided attention.

"The reason we even considered hiring your com pany, Ms. Foster, was because you assured us that one of your functions was to take care of all extraneous problems so that our negotiations could proceed smoothly. This morning I was with Mr. Windsor when he made two telephone calls to your office with the desire to have you assist him in buying his mother a birthday present. It seems she collects antique candlesticks, and he naturally assumed that you were the logical one to accompany him, since he has no idea where to shop. He was most annoyed to hear that he was being passed on to someone else on your staff. In fact, he was upset enough to terminate our talks for the day. If we lose him as a client, *we* will be the ones who will be most annoyed.

"Now, I'm certain that your staff is very capable. But Mr. Windsor is a *very* important client, and I see no reason why he shouldn't have the best, which I assume is you. Am I making myself clear, Ms. Foster?"

As if etched in stone, Ellen wanted to reply. In other words, cater to Mr. Windsor's wishes, or there'll be no contract. Did this prissy man have any idea how far his client wanted that catering to go? Remembering Gower's vinegary wife, she doubted it. She felt like a Christian being thrown to the lions, without a weapon for defense.

"I'm sorry about the mix-up, Mr. Gower. I'll call Mr. Windsor, apologize, and compile a list of good stores that deal in antiques. If he wants me to go with him, I'll be happy to do so."

"Fine, fine! I knew you would understand when the situation was explained to you. He did say he was returning to his hotel, so I'm certain you can reach him there now."

Ellen's hand shook as she replaced the receiver. How could her skin feel so cold when internally she was on fire? She'd done her best to neutralize what was between Kane and her, but now she had to accept that it was all out of her hands. She'd continue to fight the attraction—it was necessary for her company's reputation to do so—but she was horribly certain that all her efforts would only be a delaying action. An equally horrible certainty was that a small but growing part of her was awaiting the outcome with eagerness.

"Mr. Windsor? This is Ellen Foster of Foster Executive Services." Why wasn't his line busy now, when she needed more time to build some defense system?

There was a slight pause before he answered. "And what can I do for Ellen Foster of Foster Executive Services?"

Damn him! She could imagine the mocking lift to his dark brow and the laughter lurking in his eyes. But she deserved that reaction after her stilted opening. They had kissed, for heaven's sake. They had been on the brink of making love in this office. She tore her gaze from the spot before the door where their passions had soared.

"Mr. Gower called, and I must apologize for any problems you may have had this morning when your calls were routed to one of my assistants. I was extremely busy and thought she could help you with any request you might have." *Liar!* But she wasn't about to inform him that she was running scared.

"I understand that you are looking for antique candlesticks for your mother. We do have a list of reputable stores. Shall I send it to you?"

"Only if it's attached to your hand." The suggestive note in his voice changed abruptly to a note of concern. "Ellen, have you taken the time to have lunch today?"

Her glance slid guiltily to the drying ham sandwich on her desk with only one bite taken from it. "Of course. And I'll appreciate it if you don't browbeat my staff anymore."

He brushed aside her comment. "There are two calls I have to make, but I should be at your office within the hour. My mother's birthday is the day after I

91

arrive home, which is why we'll have to concentrate on getting her present."

Ellen fumed. Just like that, he expected her to shift priorities and jump at his command! Her rebellion collapsed like a punctured balloon. Gower had been explicit enough about her duties where Kane was concerned. If she wanted their contract, she had no choice but to do whatever Kane wanted. Kane had won another round.

Her eyes narrowed as an ugly thought rooted and grew. Had Kane manipulated Gower into applying pressure on her? She knew well how determined he was when he wanted something enough. To have succeeded in business to the extent that he had, he must have developed many ways to push and shove.

He wanted her. Every fiber in her alerted her to that fact. That she wanted him too was beside the point. If he hurt the reputation of her company, she would never forgive him. She carefully reviewed her conversation with Gower. Only after finding nothing to support her concern did she expel a sigh of relief. Was she searching too hard for something to impair Kane's image? All she had to do was remember how formidable he could be when crossed, how demanding and unyielding he was when his mind was set. And, oh yes, how wonderful it was to have his arms around her with her body melding to his, how his kisses drained yet exhilarated her, addicting her like a drug.

He arrived in little over a half-hour. Ellen looked at him warily as he stood in her doorway. She experienced a moment of vertigo as if she were deprived of air. Certainly it was physically impossible for him to draw the breath from her lungs from that distance!

"I see you finished your calls in plenty of time." Did he always fill the doorway so completely that he was all she could see?

92

"I decided one of them could wait until tomorrow." His father might not agree, but he'd be in better position tomorrow to tell him about his progress with their investments. After being told the second time that Ellen was unavailable, Kane had left Gower unhappy, and he himself had been blind angry over how easily she could ruin his concentration. The fact that their negotiations involved several hundred thousand dollars had lost its importance.

"There's a good selection of antiques shops on Fifty-seventh Street between Sixth and Lexington," she informed him. "I'm certain you'll find something in one of them." Her smile was politely cool as she reached for her bag. If she was lucky, she might manage to keep this afternoon on a professional level.

Ellen loved browsing in antiques shops, and she soon forgot her intention to keep her guard firmly in place. Kane, she discovered, knew a great deal about various objects, and together they admired, shook their heads over, or laughed at some of the collectibles. All the stores had candlesticks, and she was amused that he frequently knew more about a particular item than the dealer did.

From Kane, she learned that the earliest candlesticks were called prickets because, instead of being placed in sockets, candles were impaled upon thin iron spikes.

"Considering that the primitive handmade tapers lacked uniformity, it was a logical solution to keep them upright," he informed her. "It wasn't until after the Middle Ages that sockets became popular, and even then the candles had to be pared down or surrounded in wrapping to fit the size of the socket."

"One learns the darnedest things when one listens," Ellen quipped, secretly enjoying his enthusiasm. "I didn't realize you were such a font of information on the subject."

"You would be too if you had a mother who had one of the most outstanding antique candlestick collections in the country," he explained. "She has hundreds of them."

"What does she do with them?"

"You learn to weave between them," he answered with a laugh. "She's a firm believer in displaying everything she owns. People tend to be a little overwhelmed at first."

A rumble rolled over them, obliterating for the moment the traffic noise. "It looks like we're in for rain," he muttered as they glanced up at the darkening sky. "Let's try this store. It might have enough to keep us occupied until it blows over."

Kane found a silver and gold masterpiece to examine. It was the first one that attracted his attention, and Ellen wandered off so she wouldn't disturb him while he decided if it would please his mother. Spying an antique desk, she paused to check it out. Maybe she'd find one that pleased her eye—and pocketbook —in place of the Sheraton that she was longing to make her own.

Sitting on the corner of the inlaid top was a small brass candlestick, and she picked it up to examine it idly. It was crudely made, nothing like the elegant piece that Kane was interested in, but it had a certain charm that caught her attention. A pricket was welded into the center of the socket, and she wondered how many candles had been impaled on the sharp point. Her finger ran along a series of raised dots that circled the base. Realizing that they didn't follow a set design, she looked at them with curiosity. It took several minutes before she deciphered the faint impressions: SARAH + JOSEPH, 2/2/1702. Who was the long-ago

Joseph? Had he made this candleholder for his bride, laboriously hammering in the legend with a nail for all posterity?

"Kane, look, you have to see this." She hurried to him, tilting the brass holder so he could read the faint inscription. "You must admit this is one of a kind! Can't you see this Sarah using it? Each time it would be like lighting a votive candle affirming their love."

His look was quizzical as he gazed at her face. "So there *is* a romantic under that sophistication," he murmured as he examined the holder further. "I do believe you're correct. I'm certain my mother doesn't have one like this."

The purchase was quickly made, and they left the store with the package tucked under his arm. They had traveled only a few feet when the first raindrops spattered on them. A quick glance found no cruising taxis in sight.

"Come on," he said, taking her arm and urging her along. "If we hurry, we can make that tavern down the street before we get wet."

CHAPTER EIGHT

The tavern was built to look like an old English pub, which went along with the ambience created by the antiques shops that lined the street. The walls were stained dark mahogany, and the atmosphere was cozy. It was odd that she'd never noticed it before. She'd have to remember to add it to her file in case a visitor from the British Isles had a touch of homesickness.

Her eyes lit up when the menu advertised hot scones and clotted cream. She ordered it with tea, which came steeped and without a teabag in sight. "I consider this research for my company," she explained with hungry anticipation.

Kane nodded approval after tasting his tankard of bitters. "The last time I had English beer was at the Lamb and Fox in London. For your record, this tastes authentic. They must import it from England."

"And these scones are superb. You must have some." She lathered cream and strawberry jam on a section of the biscuit and offered it to him. His fingers curled around her wrist to guide her hand to his mouth. After chewing a second, he nodded his approval. Keeping his ebony eyes fastened on hers, he slowly licked the trace of cream and jam from her thumb and finger.

The velvety touch was nearly her undoing. Her knife clattered unnoticed to her plate as each moist lick sent shivers through her body. *No!* the wail reverberated silently within her. She wasn't going to let him do this to her, but she was aghast to discover that she hadn't the strength to pull away.

"Classify this as research," he suggested with a wicked smile. "I had to find out if your fingers tasted as sweet as your mouth." Her thumb disappeared into his mouth and his tongue wrapped around it, leaving Ellen to wonder if it was possible to die from the sensations tumbling through her.

There was a look of satisfaction in her dark eyes as she slowly withdrew her finger. That was a small payback for the upheaval she was creating in his life. For him, this was supposed to be a routine business trip. Although he always took feminine diversions in his stride, this woman was proving altogether too disruptive.

Last night he'd walked out of the play after the second act, although it had received rave reviews. Visions haunted him of this silver-eyed witch enjoying a meal with another man, a man she might later invite back to her apartment. He'd been pole-axed by her kisses, and experience told him that anyone with as much banked passion as she had wasn't about to say good-bye to an escort at the door. For the short week that remained, he intended that that passion would be his alone. A moment's uneasiness over the force behind that possessive assertion touched him. He shrugged it away, telling himself it was his *modus operandi.* When involved with a woman, it was understood that there was no sharing.

And there was no doubt in his mind that he wanted this woman.

At first he'd been distantly amused by her fierce resolve against any form of fraternization. Now he was discovering enchantment every time he heard her laugh. Then there were those silver eyes, which changed with remarkable frequency. Each expression brought a color shift that he found he was cataloguing with increasing interest.

He was primarily a man's man, but he admitted to enjoying exchanging opinions with this successful and dedicated career woman. With each shared laugh, each intense rebuttal, he discovered another facet of her personality that intrigued him. He found himself looking forward with increased anticipation to the final unveiling of the inner person. A man wouldn't get tired of having this woman sit across from him breakfast after breakfast.

Ellen thanked him for his gift of her own personal train, and he repeated his offer. "When my mother found out my basement was large enough to hold the collection I had when I was a kid, she sent them over. My nephews are older now and can enjoy them, so I plan to have the trains set up for Christmas. That invitation to come and play with them remains open for you too." Ellen smiled wistfully at the thought as their conversation shifted to other subjects.

They were arguing a moot point over whether Atlantis had ever existed—how in the world did they ever get off on that subject, Ellen wondered in amusement—when Kane stopped in midsentence to stare with an eyebrow raised at a booth on the far side. He continued with their discussion, but her curiosity was aroused. She poured the remainder of the tea into her cup before she glanced casually over her shoulder.

Her teeth bit into her lower lip in surprise. Tom Gower! What was he doing here—checking on her conduct? He had some nerve, considering that it was because of his order that she was here catering to his client!

The woman with him leaned forward, and Ellen saw

the reason for Kane's raised eyebrow. The curves on the woman had no resemblance to the angular shape of his wife. In fact, the blond hair and the emerald green dress could never be confused with anything the pursed-lipped Florence Gower, daughter of Archibald Little, senior partner of Little and Gower, and vehement crusader on the question of moral values, would wear.

"Hoo-boy!" Ellen whispered. The fatuous smile on Gower's face told its story.

She turned back to Kane and caught the sardonic amusement in his eyes. "A cousin, perhaps?" he asked straightfaced.

"Very doubtful. He couldn't possibly be related to anyone as ripe-looking as that!"

He cocked his head to further study the more-than-adequate curves of the woman. "I don't know. There's such a thing as recessive genes."

"I've heard of miracles, but there's a limit to what can be expected from those poor chromosomes."

"Well, what next? We'll have to pass them on our way out. Do we brazen it out and stop to say hello?"

She stared at him in disbelief. "Are you out of your mind? Once he knows that I've seen him, I can kiss good-bye any hope for their signature on that contract."

Her mouth snapped shut, and she stared at him warily. Now she'd done it. Once Kane knew how important that contract was to her, he'd have ammunition to use against her. Would he use it to force her to play his game? If only she knew more about him! Was she so defensive where he was concerned that she felt the need to blacken his character?

"The rain has stopped, but we could order a drink and wait them out. Or would you like more tea?" he suggested. He seemed amused by the situation, and it helped ease her tension. *They* weren't the ones doing anything that needed hiding. Unfortunately, it was Gower who held the cards where that contract was concerned. It was to her advantage to play her hand very carefully.

The waitress stopped by Gower's booth, and Ellen breathed a sigh of relief as a glance over her shoulder revealed that he was paying for their drinks. They slipped from the booth, and Gower picked up a fur coat that lay on the seat next to the woman. He draped the mink around her shoulders, and she gave a self-satisfied giggle while snuggling her face in the soft pelts.

The coat looked so new that Ellen wouldn't have been surprised to see the pricetag still on it—but furs on a warm summer day? *Don't be dense,* she chided. Who looked a gift horse in the mouth? She couldn't help recalling the luscious Rita Garcia fondling her two-carat diamond, and the sardonic lift to Kane's black brow as he wrote the check. There were ways, and there were ways, to pay for services rendered.

The fun had drained from the day, and she arose determinedly from her seat. "They're gone now, so we might as well leave," she announced coolly.

He stared at her through narrowed eyes as he placed several bills on the table. What had brought on this change? It must have been seeing those two. Of all the places in Manhattan to stop for a drink, why did Gower have to bring his woman here?

While Kane searched for a cab, Ellen's gaze wandered down the street. She discovered that Gower and his friend had gone to the corner and had better luck. The door slammed shut, and their taxi proceeded along the one-way street toward them.

Ellen attempted to shrink behind Kane, but he had her by the waist as he flagged down a cruising car. His

100

action caught Gower's attention as his taxi swept by. If it weren't so fateful, Ellen would have laughed at Gower's horrified expression.

They were still standing in front of the tavern, and Gower surely must suspect that they had seen him in there with his companion. Ellen's shoulders slumped in resignation. She knew Gower's type well enough to realize that the incident would probably produce repercussions. Would he dare hold the unsigned contract over her as a threat to keep her mouth shut? Of course, *she* could use the information to make certain that it was signed. But was saving her dream so important that she would actually do that? At the moment she couldn't say.

"Did Frances Agee get off safely this morning?" Ellen asked after Kane gave her address to the driver. She liked the woman and still felt slightly guilty about her illness. "She looked restless and ready to leave when I saw her yesterday."

"Unfortunately, she's still there. Last night she had some kind of reaction to one of the medications. She's all right now," he said quickly when he heard Ellen's soft gasp of concern. "Her flight reservations were changed to tomorrow morning. She threatens to be on that plane even if she has to sign herself out. By the way, she mentioned that she enjoyed your visit. What's this about a franchise of your company in Toronto?"

"She was intrigued by what we do, so I gave her a quick rundown of the business."

"Are you trying to steal her from my staff?"

"Of course not! If you remember, she told you that her husband refused to let her travel with you anymore. As a result, she's concerned about her job. From there the conversation went to what I was doing."

He frowned. "She has something there. But frankly,

I'm tired of having to break in a new secretary every few months."

"Maybe your luck would be better if you hired an older woman," Ellen suggested. "Someone who didn't have a jealous husband and who wasn't looking for, er, extra-curricular benefits."

"You mean like Bella?" he asked silkily, annoyed by her innuendo.

"Oh, no you don't! Bella is mine!"

His chuckle left her wondering. If Kane offered Bella a great deal of money, would she be tempted to make the move?

"Those scones you had don't count as a meal," Kane said as the taxi turned down her street. "I've canceled the theater tickets and will be around for you at eight. After dinner, I'd like to investigate a night-club that I hear plays something besides rock." *Where I can finally hold you in my arms.*

He quickly silenced her objection. "I'm not letting you hide behind that rule about fraternization. You as much as admitted that Tom Gower ordered you to make sure my visit remains pleasant. Pleasant means having dinner with you, and then going dancing with you. Certainly you can't find fault with that simple request."

Ellen could think of many reasons to do just that. Such as that sitting in the enclosed confines of a cab concentrated his magnetism so she had to struggle not to close the small gap separating them and lean into his warmth. She was not looking forward to being held in his arms on a dance floor. How was she going to prevent making a spectacle of herself if her legs buckled, as they had the annoying habit of doing when she was that close to him?

He helped her to the sidewalk and glanced at his watch. "I had no idea it was this late. Bella will be leaving any minute, and I promised to check in with her about several calls I've been expecting. Do you mind if I use your phone?"

Ellen couldn't very well refuse, and so she gave a grudging nod. As a gambit to get her alone in her apartment, that maneuver rated high marks.

There was a message, and it was that he call Mr. Bigelow. They had an appointment for eleven the next morning. Bigelow wanted it to be rescheduled to nine. Kane agreed, and only after he replaced the receiver did he recall his previous commitment.

"Dammit. I wasn't thinking. I forgot that I have to take Frances to the airport at ten tomorrow."

"That's no problem. That's one of the services we provide," Ellen reassured him. "I'll be happy to see that she gets on the plane."

Kane smiled. "I'm beginning to see that Frances has a point. We could use a branch of your company in Toronto. And Windsor Enterprises will be the first customer."

Two steps brought him to her. His lips were a light brush that still managed to burn. The tip of his tongue cooled the heat on the next pass. The contrast created an incredible ache in Ellen that was assuaged only when he took full possession of her mouth. Then other, incredible aches started throbbing throughout her body, building with each pulsing beat to pour through her.

He tasted faintly bitter from the beer, but beyond that was *him*, this stunning man. He was the only person who had ever managed to do these remarkable things to her.

"Is there a reason I have to leave?" he murmured as her eyelids were sealed with soft kisses.

His hand splayed sensually around her throat. His fingers extended to dip under the neckline of her dress, and Ellen was caught in a struggle against the assault on her senses. "You'd better go. I have to shower and dress for dinner," she breathed in a strangled gasp.

He paused in his gentle assault on her earlobe. "You have to undress first before dressing," he whispered huskily into her ear. "And you'll discover that I'm very versatile in the shower."

"I have no doubt." She was spinning on an upward spiral, and if his seduction weren't halted immediately, it would be too late. From somewhere she managed to find the strength to arch her back to put space between them. "I really prefer that you leave."

His hand was low on her hip, pulling her lower body to his. "Why are you fighting this?" he asked in surprise. "You know we're going to become lovers. Is there someone else? That man you wouldn't break the date with?"

Ellen refused to use poor Bob as a defense. She felt a spark of anger at his assurance that they'd end up in bed, and she grabbed it, fanning it to life. "No, there isn't someone else, but I'm not into one-night stands, or even two or three nights. Which is about the time you have here."

His lips tightened a fraction. "I'm not into them either, but conditions limit our time together. For heaven's sake, we're two healthy, normal adults. Why shouldn't we enjoy what we can give to each other?"

Why not, indeed? Ellen wondered bleakly. Her body craved the relief only he could give. Although she was highly selective, she was never one to be coy about what she wanted, and every nerve, every cell in her body cried for this man. Why then this hesitation? Because more was at stake than a night of self-indulgence, her warning system shouted.

"Are you going to force me?" she asked stonily.

His face flushed in anger, and his hands dropped slowly to his side. "I've never had to use force in my life, and I see no reason to start now."

"Then why do you keep pressuring me?"

A hard smile creased his face. "Perhaps it's because I'm intrigued. You're a challenge, Ellen Foster. As I warned you, I thrive on them. I'll see you at eight."

Seconds later, he was out of the door, and Ellen was leaning weakly against it for support. Was he right, was some part of her actually challenging him? Surely he was putting his own interpretation on her very real reason for resisting his advances. The reputation of her company was vitally important to her. Hadn't she fired one person for succumbing to a client's seduction? Was she to be as weak as Peggy had been? At the time, she'd condemned her conduct, but since coming up against Kane Windsor, she could understand why the woman had capitulated.

By the time Kane returned, Ellen had her defenses well in place, with a full range of artillery on the ready. The trouble was that Kane acted charmingly diffident, as if all he were interested in was having a pleasant evening with an attractive woman. Their conflict of only a few hours before might never have been. Evidently he had accepted her refusal to play his game.

The restaurant he selected was elegant, the food superb, and the conversation stimulating. Without her even being aware of it, Ellen's guns were discarded one by one until only the unguarded walls were left.

Nightclub was too ambitious a name for Johnny's. Still, the club had a certain atmosphere that met with their approval. As the trumpet sobbed and the trombone mourned a rendition of an old blues melody, Ellen discovered that dancing in Kane's arms was the perfect way to pay homage to the song.

"Did I tell you how lovely you look tonight?" he

murmured in her ear as the trumpet cried its farewell to love.

"No, and you were very remiss."

"Then accept my humble apologies." The first night she'd stunned him with her slinky black dress, then she had amused him with her virtuous cover-up the next evening. Tonight she'd chosen a deceptive sea-green gown that stated simply, *I am woman.*

She raised her head from his shoulder to give him a mocking look. "Somehow I can't see you being humble about anything."

He had to admit that he couldn't either. But since meeting this woman, he'd become acquainted with even that sensation. Perhaps it was part of the challenge, as was the way her kisses caused his knees to want to buckle. True, at times he felt it would be safest to drop his pursuit and run, but he brushed the idea aside. There was nothing to be concerned about in this small dalliance. It spiced his time here. After all, he'd experienced it all where women were concerned. With only eight days to go, what danger could she be to his well-organized life?

CHAPTER NINE

"What do you think of the scandal at Tomas and Brown?" Jeanne asked from the doorway after her boss had arrived the next morning, Friday.

Ellen dropped her purse into her drawer before looking questioningly at her assistant. "I didn't know there was one."

Jeanne stared at her in surprise as she came into the office. "Where have you been since yesterday afternoon? It broke on the six o'clock news and rated the first page of this morning's *Times.*" She placed the folded newspaper on the desk and pointed to the corner column.

Tomas and Brown was an investment house much like Little and Gower, although it hadn't been in the business as long. Grover Brown, it seemed, had been manipulating the investors' money and had taken off to parts unknown with two million dollars tucked under his arm, along with his secretary.

Ellen finished reading the article and snorted in disgust. "The fool! Does he really think he'll get away with that?"

"He evidently intends to give it a good try," Jeanne said pointedly while examining the photo of the sallow-faced man. "I wonder what his secretary saw in him. He doesn't look like much, but I guess two big ones can make anyone look good."

"Cynicism doesn't become you," Ellen said. "What I'm concerned about is how this will effect other investment companies. Can you imagine the panic it could create in their houses?"

From experience, she knew that whenever something unfortunate like this hit the news, it invariably started repercussions throughout the industry. Investors tended to look for other places to multiply their money. Would Little and Gower be caught in the bind? And more important, would the slowdown in business cause them to review her contract as an unnecessary expenditure until the scare subsided?

"I wonder how much of this sort of thing goes on that we never even hear about," Jeanne mused. "I wouldn't be surprised if a lot gets covered up if the money loss isn't too large. No company could survive without the confidence of its clientele."

Ellen froze as images flashed through her mind of a mink coat and the fatuous look on Tom Gower's face as he placed it across the blonde's shoulders. Had the money for that expensive gift come out of his own pocket, or had the company an unwitting contributor? If that was so, how safe was Kane's money in that man's hands?

She almost wanted to locate Bigelow's number and call Kane with a warning. But that was a great way to be laughed at. Just because her imagination was taking over didn't make Gower some kind of villain. He was simply playing around outside of his marriage. Considering the number of married men who had tried to date her, there was nothing novel about that. She managed to push away the unpleasant sensation that all was not right by focusing on her itinerary for the day.

"I've notified Ralph to have the limo ready. I have to pick up Frances Agee at the hospital and take her to

LaGuardia," she announced. "If anything comes up, I'll leave it to you to cope with it."

Jeanne was proving to be invaluable for handling the innumerable problems that crept up in this highly personalized business. Ellen had even attempted to talk her into taking the managerial position in one of the new offices, in Atlanta or Dallas, but she was a New Yorker and had said flatly that she had no desire to live any place other than in the Big Apple.

The morning rush hour was over, and the traffic was at its usual glut. Ellen was thankful that Ralph was at the wheel and she could relax. Last night she and Kane had danced until one o'clock. By then she had been floating in some magical universe where there existed only the two of them and the exquisite torture that they were performing on each other as they danced. Their hands caressed and smoothed; their thighs moved as one with each step in a tantalizing foreplay. If they'd been dancing in her living room, Ellen knew that their clothes would have long been gone, and the ungodly ache building in them would have found satisfaction.

By one, Kane had had enough and called for the check. When they'd waited for the taxi, she knew it was only a case of "your place or mine." Unfortunately, or fortunately, the cab driver had been in a garrulous mood and kept up a monologue about the inadequacy of the city's government, about barbaric out-of-state drivers, and about the graft-ridden police who didn't clear the streets of trucks so a hard-working man could make an honest buck.

The seats were uncomfortable, and the interior smelled as if it were lined with old cigar butts and empty whiskey bottles. By the time they reached Ellen's apartment, their sweet soaring had succumbed to

109

the harsh realities of life. Both of her feet were back firmly on solid ground.

Kane must have sensed that the euphoria was gone, because his tip to the driver had been an insult. Knowing how generous he was usually, she knew it was an adequate gauge of his disgust.

He took her key and opened the door before handing it back to her. He followed her inside and closed the door with his foot before halting her with a hand on her arm.

He turned her slowly to him and cupped her face with tender roughness. "That man should be drawn and quartered," he stated grimly as he searched her face for any lingering sign of the dreamy passion that had softened it while they were dancing. She gazed at him warily, and he let out a sigh. He could see that the walls were firmly in place.

"We both know I can take you in my arms and kiss away all those barriers you like to erect between us. But then later, you'll cry coercion and use it to build another, bigger barrier. You felt my body's response to you while we danced, so you know how much I want to make love with you. But not under those conditions. You'll notice I said make love with, not to you. I want you to come to me with no reservations, when your need is so strong that only the two of us is what matters. However, I want to remind you that you have only seven days to come to terms with what's between us."

His thumb rubbed her lower lip as he spoke, but then it was replaced by his mouth. He'd kissed her before with more passion, more hunger. He'd also been more demanding and persuasive. But this kiss was gentle, yet evocative, a promise of what could be, and was even more devastating to her senses because

110

she wanted what he offered but knew she couldn't have it.

As Ralph tried to pace the traffic lights, Ellen remembered Kane's words, words that only fed the ache that wouldn't quit. Seven days he was giving her to come to him. She had to think of it as seven days until he was gone and her life could get back on track.

"There's never any parking near a hospital," Ralph informed her when they reached St. Clare's Hospital on the west side. "I'll let you out at the entrance and keep circling the block until you come out."

"I'll try to make it as quick as possible," Ellen promised. Her sophisticated-career-woman facade was firmly in place by the time she rode the elevator to the eighth floor where Frances was waiting. It was a facade that she'd worked hard to achieve and that was now easy to assume. It annoyed her considerably that it cracked in the presence of a certain Canadian; only then was the vulnerable woman beneath it exposed. The remaining days of Kane's visit couldn't pass quickly enough for her.

"It's very kind of you to come for me," Frances said as the limousine left the dankness of the Queens Midtown Tunnel and picked up the Long Island Expressway leading to the Brooklyn-Queens Expressway. The route would take them to LaGuardia Airport.

"I could say this is all part of the service, and it is, but beyond that I'm glad for the opportunity to see you again." It was the truth. Ellen liked the woman.

"You have no idea how much I've been thinking about running an escort service like yours." The secretary's pale cheeks were delicately flushed as she flipped open a notebook, displaying reams of notes. "If I do check into the work you outlined, and it looks

111

feasible to open one in Toronto, will you consider selling me a franchise?"

Ellen stared at her in amazement. "You really are interested, aren't you? When Mr. Windsor mentioned that you talked about it, I thought that you were playing with the idea because you were bored."

"Did he sound angry?" she asked guiltily. "I wasn't going to tell him about our conversation, but when he came, my bed was covered with notes and he asked what I was doing."

"He admitted that he needs someone free to travel. He's considering hiring someone older next time."

Her lips twisted in a wry expression. "I should feel awful. It's an excellent job and I enjoyed working with him, but I always had a desire to go out on my own. The trouble was, I never found anything that I wanted to devote all my energy to until you sold me on managing an escort service."

"Is that what I did?" Ellen asked with a small laugh. "If it's that easy, maybe I should really branch out with this franchise idea." All she needed was to clone herself so that she had the time. But maybe with Jeanne in charge at the home office—? Possibilities whirled, but they had to be put on hold as Ralph pulled in front of Air Canada and transferred Frances's luggage to a waiting porter.

A feeling of sadness touched Ellen as Frances disappeared down the connecting walkway to the plane. Every once in a while she met someone with whom she knew, given time, that a friendship could develop, but circumstances with Frances were such that it couldn't be. The chances were that once Frances saw the staggering amount of preparation involved before the first client could be solicited, her enthusiasm about starting a branch in Toronto would fade.

When Ellen arrived back at the office, Sue handed

her a small stack of pink slips and she glanced at the messages. One was from Bob and the others seemed minor, but one sent a small jolt through her, and she sank into the chair behind her desk and stared at it in consternation. What pressure was Tom Gower going to try this time?

She'd been so wrapped up in her continually shifting reactions to Kane that she'd forgotten yesterday's episode in the tavern. Again she recalled Gower's horrified expression when he saw her as his taxi sped by them and he realized that she was aware of his extramarital affair. Surely he didn't think she would use the incident as blackmail to assure her contract? But considering that he himself wasn't above trying some arm-twisting, he no doubt assumed she would do the same. Resentment grew with her anger. It was dog-eat-dog out there, but she had always prided herself on her integrity.

She pulled the phone closer and punched out his number. His secretary put her through at once as she worked to neutralize her anger.

"Ah, Ms. Foster, I almost gave up on your returning my call."

His manner put her teeth on edge and she answered warily, "I was taking Mr. Windsor's secretary to the airport—at his request."

"Good, good. I called because I hoped that you were free to have lunch with me today. There are several business matters I wish to discuss."

I bet! "I can be free by one. Will that be all right with you?"

"Fine, fine. Do you know Poston? It's a small place about halfway between our offices."

"I know the place. I'll see you at one."

Now what will this be about? she wondered as she replaced the receiver. Her suspicions seemed to have some basis: Whatever he was plotting, he was shying away from discussing it in his office. Common sense warned that his mink-wrapped girl friend was the likely subject.

Poston was a small restaurant that served fast meals to those on the run. Considering its proximity to both their offices, Gower evidently didn't care if they were recognized, which was slightly reassuring. It removed the cloak-and-dagger aspect from their meeting. Perhaps she'd done the man a disservice. Perhaps his meal with that woman had only been a business lunch after all. Still, the question remained: Why?

When she arrived, she discovered that Gower had commandeered a table in the far corner. A glance at her watch showed that it was exactly one o'clock, reassuring her that she wasn't late. A half-empty glass of what looked like a double Scotch was on the table. She was a veteran of too many of these lunches. She knew that the fact that he was here first and needed that drink indicated how unsettled he was about the course he planned to follow. Giving a mental shrug, she threaded her way around the tables. Her professional smile was in place when he rose to greet her.

By the time she was seated, the waitress was in attendance with a menu. A button pinned to her chest advertised POSTON MEANS FAST SERVICE, and she was there to prove it. After a quick glance, Ellen ordered a fruit salad and a glass of Chablis. Gower added another double Scotch to his order for a hot roast beef sandwich.

There was nothing pretentious about the long, narrow room. Paper placemats and napkins were the only adornment to the row of tables that lined both walls. Gower's lips twisted in disdain before he took a mouthful of his drink. "I usually do better than this, my dear, but we're both busy people."

There was that detested "my dear" again, but Ellen managed to keep her smile in place. "This is fine. The food is good. And as you said, we're both busy people."

"Mm, yes." He seemed to have run out of conversation, and he drained his drink.

The waitress replaced it with a fresh one and placed the wine before Ellen. She raised the glass to her lips to hide the mocking smile. He looked ill at ease, and she felt vindictive enough to admit that that made her feel good. He'd had no compunction about putting the screws to her over Kane. If he'd kept out of it, they wouldn't have been in a position to catch him with his pants down. She grimaced over that very apropos phrase.

"I'm, um, glad you were able to help Mr. Windsor today by taking his secretary to the airport," he began.

"It's all part of our service, as I've explained."

"Um, yes. Were you successful in assisting him yesterday? He seemed to be quite concerned about finding an adequate gift for his mother's birthday."

Ellen thought of Kane's pleasure when he paid for the candlestick. The afternoon had held more enchantment than she cared to admit. "He seemed to like what he bought."

He finished most of his drink and his waffling suddenly ceased. His pale yellow eyes were hard chips of glass as he stared at her. "Is that all he bought? I happen to know that you were in a place called Johnny's. I believe it was one o'clock when Mr. Windsor managed to separate his body from yours so that you could continue elsewhere. I don't know how successful I will be in keeping my wife from passing that bit of information on to her father."

The blood receded from Ellen's face, leaving her ashen. The two-faced bastard! He had had them followed. He was actually so frightened that she might tell someone about his mink-clad friend that Gower was stooping to blackmail. She fought the urge to toss the remaining wine in his face. "If you had had the foresight to follow us, you would have found out that Mr. Windsor left after seeing me to my apartment. As for dining and dancing with him, if you recall, you gave me explicit instructions that I was to see that his stay is agreeable."

His smile was cold and empty. "When Mr. Windsor called this morning, he assured me that he was ready to come to an agreement when we meet tomorrow."

It was a Mexican standoff, and they both knew it. If there were no mention of minks, Mr. Little would hear nothing to shock his out-of-date concept on morals.

After rearranging the fruit in her salad, Ellen finally gave an excuse of a pressing appointment and managed to leave the hateful man to his double-Scotch lunch. His sandwich had not appealed to him either, she noticed.

Ellen felt dirty, used, unclean. Even the exhaust fumes from the traffic that filled the air and her lungs were preferable to how he had left her feeling. She walked the two blocks to her office, wishing it were longer so that her fury, her disgust, would have had a chance to dissipate.

How dare that self-righteous twit threaten her! She was free to indulge in an affair if she so wished. What awful twist of fate had caused Gower's and her paths to cross that day?

The adrenaline kept pumping through her system. She channeled it into the work piled on her desk, and she made masterful inroads, clearing away the backlog of reports. After Sue gave her the last one to sign, Ellen sat back with a sigh of relief. At least there'd be no guilt feelings about not taking work home. She'd be free to enjoy her evening with Kane.

Who was she kidding, she told herself upon entering her apartment. When she was with Kane, there was no room to worry about reports. Worrying about her ability to put brakes on her emotional reaction to him took all of her energy.

When Kane had told her on the phone that he had never been to New York's celebrated Chinatown, she suggested they have dinner there. He'd been agreeable, and she made reservations at Mon Sing, a small restaurant where she'd had several delicious meals. Knowing how irresistible it was to explore the endless tiny shops lining the streets of the small nine-block area, she wisely put on shoes with heels lower than usual. She'd mentioned that maybe he'd find a rare candlestick to add to his mother's collection, and she was looking forward to doing some browsing of her own.

She opened the door to Kane's knock. He strode in, impossibly rugged and handsome, and she pulled in a careful breath to ease the sudden tightness in her chest. One would think that by now the masculine vitality he exuded would have less of an impact on her. Instead, her nerves seemed programmed to jump to instant awareness that was almost painful in its intensity. It wasn't fair that he could look so in control of himself when her wits felt scattered to the four winds.

She stopped to watch him enter the room and quickly adjusted her assessment of his control. There was a lean hunter's look about the set of his shoulders and the angle of his jaw. The dark lights in his eyes told who the quarry was.

"I wasn't going to touch you," he stated as she took a step backward. "I was going to play it cool and concentrate on picking up some gifts in Chinatown."

He opened his arms, and Ellen found herself in them. The frustration, the anger, the long *empty* day were over. She was where she belonged, safely enclosed in his arms.

There was safety, and then there was safety, she thought vaguely as he kissed her mouth. She became a willing victim to the flames that each exploring plunge of his tongue fed. His hands, intent on discovering every curve hidden by the fabric of her clothes, brought her body to exquisite awareness of her own femininity. Although the sensations swirling through her had nothing to do with the usual conception of safety, she knew he'd permit no harm to come to her, and that was safety in its purest form.

His forehead was damp when he leaned it against hers. "What am I going to do about you, Ellen Foster?" he asked huskily. "I'm dealing with several hundred thousand dollars of the family's money, and I need a clear head. At the damnedest moments I discover myself thinking of silver blue eyes and the way they're crystal clear when you laugh and how they change to pewter when I kiss you. It shoots my concentration to hell. I'm no adolescent; I know you want me as much as I want you. When are you going to stop torturing us both this way?"

He felt her faint withdrawal, and he grimaced. "All right, I know we have this reservation, and the shops will be closed if we wait too long. But the night is long, and there's no reason why it should be empty. Remember that."

His finger touched the tip of her nose before releasing her. She reached for her purse, wondering how a threat could sound so much like a golden promise.

CHAPTER TEN

Ellen had the taxi driver drop them off across from Chatham Square at the juncture of Worth and Mott streets, which was considered to be the traditional gateway to Chinatown. Immediately her senses were assailed by the sights, the sounds, and the texture of the air that was found only in this minitown. There was an exciting ambience that never failed to pull her. She reached for Kane's hand to hurry him along. The contact became a conduit begging him to join her in her excited anticipation.

It was a call Kane was happy to answer. His body still ached with need for her, and this was an acceptable way to consume some of his restless energy. She gave a delighted laugh when a small Chinese woman hurried by with a tiny child in her arms. The child's cheeks were round and rosy and a button nose separated his shiny almond-shaped eyes. He smiled shyly in response to her laugh before burying his face in his mother's shoulder.

"Isn't he adorable?" she asked before pulling Kane along, eager to share everything with him.

He nodded in agreement, completely charmed by this new Ellen, her sophisticated mask tossed aside. This was a totally unexpected aspect of a personality that he now knew was multifaceted. Too bad he wouldn't be here long enough to search out the rest. It could be an interesting experience.

"What is this?" he asked, spying a small pagoda stall erected by the street curb.

"That is Ma Bell's gift to the Chinese people." Seeing his puzzlement, her grin widened. He examined the bright red glass-enclosed square with Chinese inscriptions under the stylized pagoda roof. "It's a telephone booth. I like to fantasize that any call I make from there will be scrambled automatically into Chinese," she said.

His grin matched hers. "Shall we try it and see?"

"Leave me my silly dreams!" she chided, ducking with him around a group of tourists with snapping cameras.

They paused by a brightly lit store window that was crowded with an unbelievable collection of ivory and jade objects and jewelry. "It's not silly, you know," he whispered in her ear as she looked over the selection of earrings.

"What?" she asked, adding to her collection of sensations the disconcerting way his breath tingled along her cheek.

"Dreams. I'm a firm believer that dreams are never silly. I usually work on mine to make them come true."

He was doing it again, making it impossible for her to breathe. "I'm afraid in this case I'd have to go to China."

Their fingers were entwined, and he brought them to his lips. "That can be arranged too. We're negotiating with China regarding some of our paper products. What better way to finalize the deal than to go there to sign the agreements? When that happens, could I talk you into coming along with me?"

Keep it light before you fling yourself in his arms and agree!
"I'll have to give it some thought. Do you think I can

120

sell a franchise to Foster Executive Services while I'm there?" She gave him an impudent grin before pulling him to the next display.

"Princess, I believe you can sell anyone whatever you set your mind to," he admitted ruefully. She was actually selling him on a life of chastity. If he wasn't careful, he might end up buying it if that life didn't include her. The idea stunned him, but he was soon caught up in her enthusiasm about the merchandise in the window, and the vagrant thought lost its impact.

Ellen decided the wisest course would be to concentrate on the colorful articles before them. Joss sticks crowded Buddhas and paper fans and there were numerous daintily painted procelain tea sets. It constantly amazed Ellen how the store owners managed to utilize every square inch of display area in their small shop fronts. From experience, she knew that inside the shop there was hardly any more space. In the back, a silk hanging invariably separated the commercial section from what she suspected was the living quarters of the proprietors. Were those rooms just as tiny and crowded? she often wondered.

The sidewalks were filled with people, all gaping at the overabundance of merchandise in the lighted shops. A group of teen-agers came out of a narrow carry-out store, laughing as they nibbled cautiously at the food they'd bought and carried in folded napkins. The tantalizing aromas reminded Ellen of the lunch she hadn't eaten when she was with Gower, and her stomach grumbled in protest.

The restaurant was on the next street. They climbed the flight of stairs, their fingers remaining interlocked until the waiter held the chair for her. That clasp had become so natural that she hated to let go. Kane must have felt the same unexplainable emptiness, because as soon as their orders were given, he reached for and again captured her hand.

"Tell me, did you take the time to eat a decent lunch?" he asked sternly.

"Inquisition time?" she teased. "Tom Gower called, and we met at a restaurant."

Seeing the laughter fade from her face, his own expression became hard. "Was it about that little episode we happened upon?"

She had only meant to toss in the fact that she'd been to a restaurant so that he wouldn't ask what she had eaten. It hadn't occurred to her to tell him the result of that meeting. She then recalled her reaction when she heard of the embezzlement at Tomas and Brown and her fear that Gower might be doing much the same though on a smaller scale. Would this be a way to warn Kane to be on guard about investing his family's money with this man?

"Yes," Ellen replied bitterly, and she told Kane what had happened. She hadn't realized how much that meeting had bothered her until she felt her relief after Kane extracted the story.

"You mean he's threatening not to sign the contract unless you keep your mouth shut?" His expression was incredulous.

Ellen nodded, startled by the anger simmering behind his question. "You've got it," she admitted wearily. She was tired of the whole setup. Tired of the necessity of that contract, the harassment, the fine line she had had to walk ever since Kane had come on the scene. Tired mostly that the necessity of retaining Gower's good will forced her to fight the enchantment growing between Kane and her when every part of her cried to succumb.

His clasp became almost painful. "You can stop worrying. You'll get that signed contract." He saw her wince and eased the tight grip with a muttered apology. "We can't have Foster Executive Services get into trouble just because Gower has a thing about mink-draped blondes, now can we?"

His hard smile didn't reach his eyes, and Ellen suddenly felt sorry for Gower. She wouldn't want that expression focused on her. Yet perversely it gave her a warm glow. She never before had met a man willing to take on her problems.

"Thanks for your offer, but you don't have to get involved," she protested softly. "I can manage on my own."

"I know you can, but you were with me at the time you saw Gower, and that makes it my problem also."

"Are you always so—caring?" she asked gently.

His eyes softened and took on a warm glow. "Princess, just give me a chance, and I'll be happy to show you just how caring I can be."

The tingling was there again, all the way up her arm and down to the center of her being. "That's what I'm afraid of."

"No. Never be afraid with me. Surely you must know that, the way I feel, it's impossible for me to hurt you."

His eyes blazed, and her need to touch him became an acute pain. She ached to brush his cheek, to soften the firm line of his mouth with her finger. Her tongue circled her dry lips, and she was surprised by the suppressed groan that came from him.

"I'm certain you'd never hurt me intentionally," she admitted. Her whispered statement hung between them as the waiter served the shark fin soup. She inhaled the delicious aroma before picking up her spoon. This conversation was dangerous. It was opening avenues to her inner vulnerability. She tasted the soup and found the subtle flavors to be superb. For now, she'd do the chef justice and focus her attention on enjoying her meal.

His words returned later when they strolled along Mott Street, this time for all the world like lovers, with their arms around each other's waists. Somewhere between his arrival at her door and their stepping into this quaint city-within-a-city, he had managed to do just what she swore he'd never accomplish. He'd stripped away her resistance to his charismatic charm.

"I haven't seen a single candlestick, have you?" Kane asked as they paused before another narrow storefront. The majority of shops were closed by now, but a few remained open to lure the late tourists.

"You're right," Ellen replied with some astonishment. "Still, they must have used candles before electricity was discovered."

"Or else they burned oil," he commented. From the varied displays, it was evident that none specialized in a single line, but this one seemed to lean more to jewelry. "Let's go in and ask. If nothing else, I can pick up some earrings for my sister."

The paisley material covering the rear door fluttered when they stepped into the shop and a small, elderly oriental man materialized behind the minuscule counter. His head bowed fractionally as he waited for them to speak.

"So sorry, no candlesticks." His reply to Kane's question came in whispers. A long thin hand waved over his display. "But we have pretty earrings and necklaces for the lovely lady. Guaranteed jade and ivory, not false like some places."

There was pride in the whispery voice, and Kane bent over the case. The selection was vast and crowded together, making it difficult to appreciate the individual beauty of the pieces. He eventually bought a jade earring and pendant set and a pair of exquisitely carved ivory earrings that Ellen assured him any woman would love to own.

"I never thanked you for seeing Frances off this morning," Kane said when they found a taxi. "She left a message for you that she arrived safely. It seems her husband is enthusiastic about her idea to open a service like yours. What's going on between you two, anyway?"

Ellen checked his expression from the corner of her eye. It looked politely inquisitive, but he was too smart to be fooled by any evasion. Besides, he already knew about his secretary's intention to quit and her interest in starting a branch of Ellen's company.

She placed her hand on his arm in entreaty. "I hope you're not angry at me. Frances was so enthusiastic, and the whole thing mushroomed before I was aware of how committed she was becoming to the idea."

He took her hand to cradle it between his palms. "I'm not enthusiastic about losing her and having to break in another secretary. But I can understand her point of view. I'll have to tell her to set up interviews for a replacement."

"A motherly type," Ellen reminded him, recalling their conversation of the other day.

"A Bella type," he teased. "I wonder what her asking price is?"

"Arg-g-gh!" she growled, pushing at his chest. "Bella's mine!"

He laughed as his arm settled around her shoulder. They stared solemnly at each other in a moment of assessment before his head lowered to take what she was eagerly offering.

His mouth was cool and faintly sweet from the fruit compote they'd had for dessert. "If you're mine, what does that make her?" he teased when he changed the angle of his mouth to further his exploration.

Was she already his? The question was superfluous as her tongue met his. The shudder rippling through him goaded her into further play. Their tongues entwined, enjoying subtle textures and tastes. Then suddenly that wasn't enough. His mouth ground over hers as he took her soaring, with quick evocative thrusts that left them breathless and with hearts pounding to the bursting point.

The taxi jerked to a stop at a traffic light, bringing a return to sanity. He relaxed his crushing hold and stared at her flushed face in bemusement. "What you do to me is unbelievable. It's a long time since I wanted to take a woman in the backseat of a car, far less in a taxi in the middle of Manhattan!"

Ellen shook her head to dispel the mental fog. "I never did," she admitted, and clarified when seeing the questioning lift to his eyebrow. "Never made love in the backseat of a car. Did I miss anything?"

He gave a delighted laugh and hugged her. "I doubt it. As I recall, it was damn awkward."

"Then I'm glad I'm past the awkward stage."

Kane raised her hand to place a kiss in her palm. It seemed to be suddenly incredibly delicate and fragile. Was he misreading the message? If so, he was in for a long night under a cold shower. He kissed each fingertip as she watched with eyes of liquid silver. He met her gaze and felt himself sinking willingly, eagerly, into the heated depth of her eyes. No, the message was clear. In his stupid arrogance, he'd demanded she come to him and had thought with that action that he'd cut his throat. But now the faint tremble in her hand sent its message, and a quiver started deep within him, meeting that vibration.

They were silent the rest of the short ride. What need was there for words when their bodies communicated on a plane that had its own language? He'd never experienced this electric exchange, which turned even the hairs on his arms into sensitive receivers. He was exquisitely aware of every breath she took, even of the sound his jacket made as it rubbed against her bare arm. Lucky jacket! But soon there'd be no material running interference, no shirt or dress, and he'd at last reach paradise with her silken body pressed against his.

His throat worked in a spasm as he swallowed. Frustration raged against tangled city traffic and crawling taxis. Somehow he had to wait it out until they reached her apartment. This first time had to be so perfect that it would wipe all previous experiences from her mind. He shied away from exploring why that was so important.

Bernie invited them in as if they were visiting royalty. Ellen barely noticed his presence. Her senses were attuned to one man only, and the pressure from his hand, which was wrapped around her elbow, was the guide she depended on to activate her movements. She was lost in a haze that made thinking impossible. Her lifeline to reality was Kane, and even that was a reality that was new to her.

As usual, her key was elusive and she finally offered her open purse to Kane in frustration. His smile was gentle as he found the key and inserted it into the keyhole. He closed the door behind them and they lasted for two steps into the living room before they were in each other's arms.

Her hands slipped under his jacket and around his waist as their mouths remained melded together. His hands moved hungrily over her back, pressing her close, in an overwhelming need to reaffirm her perfection against his body.

He reached for the zipper on her dress and halted the pull with an effort. To have any more of her exposed at this point would make it near to impossible to wait until they reached the bedroom. For the first time he truly considered making love on the floor. Anywhere, anyplace with this woman would be right. But this was the first time, and he wanted it to be perfect.

"The bedroom, which way?" he breathed as he nibbled hot kisses along her throat. The short hall from the living room had three doors off it. He knew one was the bath but didn't know which was to her room.

"To the right." She was panting.

There was an excitement in her voice that raised his libido several notches—not that he needed the added stimulation. What it did was make the cushioned carpet look even more expedient and desirable. Another time, he promised, as they entered the bedroom.

He was amazed at how his hand trembled as he slid the zipper down its track. When was the last time anticipation had affected him like this? he wondered. Surely not since the day he lost his virginity in his teens. But this was vastly different. Then he'd been involved in his own reaction. Now his concern was to their loving as special to her as he knew it was going to be to him.

Ellen heard the zipper make its long glide down the back of her dress. The air was cool against her heated skin, but the sensation was fleeting. All her awareness was centered on the exchange going on between their lips. Kisses shouldn't burn even as they sent icy tingles along her flesh, but these did, and more. They had her heart thundering in a heavy beat in an effort to circulate her blood, which was moving honey-thick through her viens.

He cupped her face with his fingertips as their mouths stoked fires that were already almost out of control. He traced with sensitive awareness the delicate angle of her jaw, the slender length of her neck.

He brushed the dress from her shoulders to explore with delicate thoroughness the satiny slope of her shoulders.

Then his hands drifted to new territory and followed the thin strap holding her bra in place. He found the clasp and opened it. The wisp of nylon and lace floated to the floor. Her breasts responded with immediate urgency. They swelled in tribute to his tender touch as he traced concentric circles until he reached the dark tips, which were already puckering for his attention.

"Kane." His name was a drawn-out whisper of need.

The lamp that she kept lit in the living room gave dim illumination in the bedroom. It was enough for him to see the flush suffusing her face. "Yes," he whispered. "I want to please you. Tell me what you want."

"You."

The raw urgency nearly cost him his control. "Then you better undress me."

Could her fingers obey orders that her mind couldn't form? No, they couldn't, she discovered very shortly. Her moan of frustration caused a chuckle to rumble in his chest. It became a sound of male mastery. He quickly finished the job that she was incapable of performing, and the rest of her clothes swiftly followed his.

At last her hands found the pleasure they yearned for and spanned the width of his broad chest. Her breasts came alive when they touched the covering of fine hair. When he gathered her so close that she could hardly breathe, she finally had the soul-deep satisfaction of feeling her imprint crushed into his long body.

The satin sheets were cool under her, and she wondered fleetingly if she'd changed them that morning in anticipation that this was how the evening would end.

How little one was aware of those subconscious desires!

Every atom pulsed for his possession, but Kane seemed intent upon endless torture. He spent seeming hours with his hands, his mouth lathing adulation to every part of her. When she thought she'd burst from need, from hunger, she grabbed his hair and pulled his mouth to hers.

"Now," she demanded with feverish urgency. "Now, before I explode!"

"Yes, now," he agreed, knowing that he couldn't last much longer either.

With one long smooth thrust, he made them one. She cried at the beauty of having him part of her, and wrapped her arms and legs around him as she met each thrust with all the strength in her hungering body. They climbed rapidly to the pinnacle—it could have been no other way after their exquisite foreplay. They met at the top with an explosion of starbursts that followed them like fire as they slowly returned to earth.

"I didn't know. I should have known. You were wonderful," she sighed.

His head nested between her breasts, and she felt his cheeks tighten in a smile. "Slightly incoherent, but shall I say, the feeling is mutual? You are one helluva woman."

She grinned into the darkness. "Careful of your language, buster. There's a lady present."

His tongue curled out and touched her nipple. "I'm well aware of it, princess," he agreed. He blew a breath over the dampened nub and noted with satisfaction how quickly it puckered. Instant reaction, and it wasn't the only response he was getting. His hips rotated in a tentative thrust, and he was pleased by her reciprocal movement.

"Kane?" The soft question held surprise.

He raised his head to look at her and met her questioning look with a grin. "As I said, you're one helluva woman. But first we better get back to the middle of the bed. These satin sheets are slippery, and we've worked our way to the edge."

Ellen ignored his warning, throwing her enthusiasm into responding to his movements. He quickly joined her, and somewhere along the climb to that pinnacle they slid off the bed to the floor with a soft thump.

Kane discovered he had been right. It made no difference where or when they made love; with her it was still one helluva experience.

CHAPTER ELEVEN

The pot was poised over Kane's cup. "More coffee?" Ellen asked, her gaze sweeping over him. The beam of Saturday morning sunlight slanting through the kitchen window gave glistening highlights to his near-black hair, still damp from the shower. His unbuttoned shirt hung loosely from the shoulders where her head had rested a short while ago. The pot wavered for a second as memories stirred.

"Top it, please." Kane pushed aside the plate stained with remnants of the eggs she'd poached for his breakfast and leaned back with a smile of satisfaction. "Mornings like this could spoil a man," he announced, and chuckled indulgently when a rosy hue stained her cheeks.

"Don't let it go to your head," she replied tartly. "I can't even remember the last time I made breakfast, far less ate like this." At his insistence, she'd also made an egg for herself and had been surprised to find she enjoyed it, as well as an English muffin. But then, she'd used up a lot of energy the evening before. The memory of how often they'd made love deepened the flush. Last night had been hers, a gift she'd treasure for a long time.

He shook his head in disgust. "You need a keeper. Anyone that expends as much energy as you do should know the body can run only so long on its reserves."

132

She looked at him askance, wondering if he was walking into her thoughts again, but his next words showed he was going in another direction.

"All nutritionists will tell you how important the first meal of the day is, especially for someone in a stressful occupation. Your gastric juices need something to work on. If you don't eat, they work on the lining of the stomach. Why do you think you have this discomfort?"

Because I knew you were coming, and I didn't know if I would be able to cope with seeing you again. The realization had her catching her breath.

He continued with added fervor. "It's because of the pressure normal to anyone in an executive position. Don't you think I'm speaking from experience? We're all potential victims, whether we recognize it or not. It's documented that the top two hazards for people in our type of jobs are ulcers and high blood pressure. So take care of yourself enough to at least eat *something* each morning, will you please?"

She braced her elbows on the table and rested her chin on her folded hands before deliberately widening her eyes as if she were hanging on to every word he said. "Yes, Daddy, I'll do my best," she agreed, trying to keep her laughter from erupting. He really was concerned!

His eyes narrowed dangerously. "If it weren't this late, I'd show you how much of a daddy I'm not!"

"It's the weekend, the time normal people rest. You could always change the appointment you have, or call in sick," she suggested, a wicked glint in her eye.

"I could also take you over my knee and show you what happens to saucy women."

Her eyes widened further. "Ooh, kinky! What else is in your repertoire?"

His smile broadened. "Let's put it this way. Was

133

there anything you didn't like last night or this morning?"

Ellen knew when she was cornered. She gathered the dishes and put them in the sink. Kane was behind her before she could turn. His arms were a protective circle around her, and she leaned into the warmth of his chest.

His breath caressed her cheek as he kissed her throat. "You know that I prefer staying here with you. I would gladly cancel out, but my appointment is with an important customer of ours who's leaving tomorrow for a vacation in Acapulco. This was the only meeting time we could work out."

Her arms crossed his, tightening his hold. "I understand. It's not like me to be selfish."

He buried his face in the warm curve of her neck, where he could inhale deeply her enticing scent. "No more selfish than I feel. I should be finished by noon. Are you free to have lunch with me?"

"Oh, yes!" she agreed eagerly.

He turned her in his arms and took total possession of her mouth in a kiss that left her limp and trembling. Sensing her weakness, he pushed her against the cabinet, using his body as a brace. It was a mistake, but a glorious one. All through the night his body had become programmed to hers, and her response now was instantaneous and predictable.

The buzzer's noise intruded, and Bernie's voice came hollowly through the intercom. "The taxi you ordered is here. Shall I hold it or let it go?"

"Something has to be done about that man's sense of timing," Kane said angrily as he released her and reached to depress the talk button. "I'll be right down, Bernie." He looked ruefully at Ellen, who was still leaning helplessly against the cabinet, as he quickly fastened his shirt. "Needless to say, I have no desire to leave, but as it is, I'll just have time to get to the hotel and change."

She followed him into the living room and held his jacket as he slipped into it. "I'll make this as fast as I can," he promised, pressing a swift, fierce kiss to her lips as he shoved his necktie into his pocket. "By the way, tonight is dress-up time. We're invited to another fancy dinner. I'll tell you all about it when I come back."

Then he was gone, and Ellen stared for long seconds at the closed door before turning to look around the room. Her apartment had vibrated minutes ago with his energy, but now it had an empty feeling about it. For heaven's sake, Kane had been here for only one night! He couldn't have left behind this strong an impression. This was her home. It was she who gave this place its vitality, not some man who would soon be but a memory.

An icy chill ran down her back. A pain started to build in her middle, and she pressed her hand against her stomach to ease the ache. So much for Kane's declaration about the importance of breakfast! She knew that egg would sit uncomfortably in her stomach.

She wandered into the kitchen to wash the dishes. Then, knowing it couldn't be put off any longer, she went into the bedroom. Satin sheets were definitely not made for the use they had been subjected to the night before. The bed looked like a battle had taken place on it. Actually, a series of skirmishes was more like it, she admitted with a wry smile. There'd been several of them, and both sides had come out winners.

She yawned while reaching for clean sheets, this time percale, and she felt the exhaustion creep up on her. They'd gotten little sleep the night before, and she hoped that Kane would manage to get through the morning and remain sharp. She stared at the pillow that still held the imprint of his head. It had seemed so right waking up with him beside her.

She yawned again, and she gave in to the need for sleep. Dropping her robe, she slid into bed. Satin sheets had their place, she admitted, loving the cool smoothness along her naked body. But Kane had a point. They were a little slippery. She grinned sleepily at private memories as her lashes drifted down to fan across her cheeks. She was unaware that she gathered his pillow into her arms and held it close to her.

A fire truck screaming down the street woke her. It took Ellen several minutes to adjust to the fact that she'd actually slept the morning away and it was almost noon. She couldn't recall the last time she'd indulged in that luxury.

Then it struck her that Kane would arrive soon, and she leaped out of bed and hurriedly changed the linen while planning what to prepare for lunch. She didn't want to go out to eat. He'd be exhausted. She was certain he'd prefer a leisurely meal and then perhaps a nap. They would both benefit from a relaxing afternoon. The pressure would return when they went to the party that evening. Ellen knew what these affairs were like. Business discussions would intrude until the party became little more than an extension of the office.

It was almost one when Bernie announced over the intercom that Mr. Windsor was on the way. She suppressed a smile. The doorman sounded like he expected her to roll out the red carpet and have trumpets announcing Kane's arrival. The way her pulse was accelerating, the idea wasn't that bad.

She answered the door at his first knock. Did he always look so sexy? she wondered, staring at him.

"Kane." It was a helpless whisper, telling of yearnings and of fears that their night together had been only a dream.

His eyes, hot black coals, remained on her as he nudged the door closed. He dropped his attaché case to the floor and swept her up in his arms.

His kiss was fierce at first, telling of his hunger, but it soon became a tender savoring of flavors and textures that needed to be explored again. "I needed that. A year is too long."

An expressive eyebrow arched as she laughed up at him. "It was only four hours," she corrected.

He nuzzled the warm curve of her neck, inhaling deeply of the essence that was this woman. "Perhaps according to your clock, but not by mine. I swear it took him a month just to say hello and discuss the convention."

"Poor baby," she murmured, her hands enjoying the luxury of once again threading through his thick shock of hair.

"I'll show you what this poor baby needs."

With a shriek, Ellen found herself lifted off the floor and being carried to her bedroom. "But I have lunch prepared."

He paused by the kitchen door. "Is anything on the stove?"

She shook her head, and he grunted in satisfaction. "Then it can wait. This is a case of first things first."

He stood her by the bed and removed her blouse before she could form a protest. *What protest?* she chided, kicking off her sandals just as he edged her slacks over her hips. His jacket, tie, and clothes landed haphazardly on the chair, and the two of them collapsed, arms and legs entwined, onto the bed.

Minutes later, embarrassment struggled with concern as he brushed a strand of hair from her damp forehead. "I'm sorry, princess. Did I hurt you? I didn't mean to come at you like an animal. I've never lost my control like this before."

She traced a finger over the red mark she'd made on his shoulder. "It's a moot point over who lost what control," she conceded contritely. "I never did anything like this before, either."

He glanced down at the curved row of teeth marks, and something hot filled his chest. She'd been as wild as he had been, meeting stroke for pounding stroke with a wantonness that had driven him beyond reason. "I'll wear my battle scar proudly."

His grin was earthy and very male, and her heart did a funny half-skip before racing to a faster beat. "Don't let it go to your head, buster. It will fade, and I'll deny everything."

"Then I better have a picture taken of it right away, so I have evidence to show to our—" The laughter faded, and he hurriedly kissed her to give reason for his abrupt pause. Good Lord, was he really about to say grandchildren? Where did that crazy thought originate? Finding this remarkable woman was simply a marvelous bonus he'd lucked into. After today, there were only four days left to enjoy her. This was simply a pause in their busy life. Then he had to return to Canada, and she'd remain in the States.

"You did say something about lunch?" he asked, releasing her and rolling on his back, his arm over his eyes.

"I'll take a quick shower first, then you can have the bathroom while I get the food ready." She was glad he wasn't looking to see how off-balance she felt. She had felt a withdrawal in his last kiss. In spite of his words, was he repelled by her wantonness? He'd come on like a pirate, tearing away all pretensions and carrying her away in the turbulence of his lovemaking. She'd responded in ways she hadn't known possible, had reveled in the wildness, in the primitive coupling.

Ellen felt raw and exposed and unable to cope. She disappeared into the bathroom with the hope that the routine of taking a shower would return her to normal.

When they finished lunch, Kane tried to hide a yawn as Ellen refilled his cup with coffee. She looked at him with sympathy. "Look, I was able to take a nap this morning, but you haven't had a chance to get any sleep. Why don't you stretch out on the bed for a while? Otherwise, you'll never make it through the evening."

"You might have something there," he agreed. "Can I talk you into taking a nap with me?"

She looked at him mockingly. "And just how much rest will you get?"

Amusement danced in his eyes. "Thanks for the compliment. However, as much as I'd like to prove it, I'm afraid I'm not superman. I bow to the inevitable. Frankly, madame, I'm pooped."

A flush rose to her cheeks, and he gave an indulgent smile. "I still would like having you with me. There's something comforting about feeling you next to me." *Careful there, Kane, old boy!* The warning was benign, and he was too tired to give it any particular notice.

Ellen quickly rinsed the dishes and followed him into the bedroom. The bed was alluring, and she had to admit that she, too, found it comforting to be next to him.

"Where is the dinner party tonight?" she asked idly as she slipped out of her blouse. She was doing a lot of dressing and undressing that day. Thinking of the reason brought a bemused smile.

Kane placed his clothes over the chair, this time with care, before pulling back the bedcovers. He stretched out on the sheets and watched with fascination as each piece of her apparel was discarded. "Didn't I tell you?" he muttered through a half-yawn as she slid in next to him. "The Littles are entertaining at their home."

Ellen reared up to stare at him in shock. "What?" she cried in disbelief. "After all I've told you about them, you're willingly placing me deeper in an already untenable position?" She scrambled to get off the bed, but his arm curved around her waist, holding her against him.

"That's exactly why I'm taking you there," he said, pressing her onto the pillow. "And if you stop struggling, I'll explain my reasons."

She stopped because he was sprawled over her, using his weight to quiet her. "So explain. This better be good!" she snapped, glowering at him.

"I admit that as a man Gower leaves me cold, and I'm not just referring to that incident we stumbled on yesterday. I'm not interested in his private life. I do have respect for the man's business sense. I've depended upon that sense myself on several occasions and realize what a valuable tool it can be. Do you realize that if I hadn't selected them, we wouldn't have had this?"

He smiled seductively. When her gaze remained stormy, he gave a small sigh before continuing. "I admit I thought you were overreacting regarding their attitude about us going out, but after listening to your story about Gower trying to pressure you, I'm seeing the error of my thoughts. I despise people who use their power that way. Especially on someone I care about." His eyes were polished jet, cold and hard, and the sight sent a shiver through Ellen.

"When Little invited me to his party, it came to me that this was an excellent opportunity to apply a few screws of my own and pull a few claws at the same time."

"But is it necessary for me to be along?" Ellen asked. Already she felt sympathy for Gower. She'd be demolished if ever Kane's ruthless expression was focused on her.

"Naturally. They hired you to see that my visit to New York runs smoothly. As far as they're concerned, that's the reason you're with me. I intend to have that bit of information branded in both Little and his wandering son-in-law's minds so they never question that fact again. While the amount of Windsor money I'm channeling through them may not be the largest account they handle, it's not one they'd like to lose. Especially since some of my Canadian friends have shown interest in them, and my recommendation will be critical in their decision."

"As usual, money speaks," Ellen muttered.

"And don't ever forget that, princess. To some people, it's the moving factor in their lives."

But not in yours, she knew intuitively. That commodity was important to grease the wheels of business, but if circumstances were different, he'd be just as happy drawing on the Indian part of his heritage, stalking animals in the wilderness and living off the land.

"Now do you forgive me?" he asked, closing her eyes with light kisses.

Her hands caressed the muscles ridging the strong arms braced on either side of her. "It's the reverse. Do you forgive me?" Now that he had explained his position, her awareness centered on his naked flesh pressed over hers.

Kane rolled from her with a rueful shake to his head. "Later, princess, when all my senses are in full working order. Making love to you is too special. I don't want to miss out on any part of it."

He pulled her into the curve of his body. It seemed a mere minute before the even cadence of his breath whispering across the back of her neck told her he was asleep. With a deep sense of contentment, she cuddled into a closer bond and joined him.

Kane's assurance was hers. Knowing the man, she had full confidence that he'd solve her problem with Gower. Incredibly, he'd even managed to erase her guilt about abdicating her stand against fraternization. Later, when he was gone, she was afraid it would return, but now she was content to accept as a gift each night that was theirs. There were so precious few left.

CHAPTER TWELVE

Kane hired a car for the evening, and they took the George Washington Bridge to New Jersey. The trip was relatively easy. Most of the weekend revelers were heading into the Big Apple, so the traffic flow was opposite to the way they were headed. Little's directions were precise, so they had no difficulty finding Englewood and the road to his house. His modest estate overlooked the Palisades, offering an impressive view of the Hudson River. Across the expanse of water, Manhattan's irregular skyline glowed with uncountable lights.

"It figures," Ellen said as she took in the Victorian outline of the large house. The gables were steep, and the gingerbread trimming was excessive, yet she admitted it had a special charm and bespoke a time when lives were led at a more leisurely pace.

"And what do you mean by that?" Kane asked as they approached the steps that led to the wide porch.

She waved her hand at the ornate facade. "Isn't it obvious? I can see now why Little has been able to cling to his archaic position on morality in spite of spending large portions of each day coping in today's business world. After an evening in this period piece, he's recharged. It's enough to immunize him against the real world."

Kane's laugh filled the night air. "You may have

something there. Since Tom is my agent, I haven't had much contact with Little. Now, after seeing this place—" He shook his head in wry acknowledgment of the truth of her perception.

The house proved to be a museum piece. Dark oriental rugs covered highly polished oak floors, and heavy maroon damask draperies obliterated the windows. The Victorian furniture was stained dark mahogany; the legs were bowed with clawed feet. The small piecrust side tables and the crowded marble mantelpiece to the fireplace made Ellen think that nothing had been changed in the room since Little's grandmother had been brought there as a bride. To her delight, there was even a floor frame in one corner holding a partially finished needlepoint canvas, which several women were admiring.

A large crowd was already assembled. Few sat on the chairs, reminding Ellen of her grandmother's furniture in the "best" parlor and how discouragingly hard the seats had been. These looked every bit as hard and uncomfortable as the ones she remembered.

Archibald Little hurried over when he saw Kane. His expression froze momentarily when he noticed who was with him, and for an instant Ellen thought that even Kane would be able to do nothing to change this man's deep-seated prejudices.

"Mr. Windsor, Ms. Foster, how good to see you!" Little said with what for him was a hearty greeting. It sounded to Ellen more like a wheeze from an old bellows. He topped Kane by an inch but was gaunt to the point of emaciation. His thin, sandy hair was liberally sprinkled with white, and the lines on his face were all vertical, giving him a vinegary appearance. "I hope my directions were adequate."

"We had no difficulty following them," Kane assured him.

Little gave a pursed-lip smile that reminded Ellen of the one she had seen on his daughter's face at the Bigelow party. "I don't believe you've met my wife, Olivia," he offered, pulling a small woman from behind him, where she had hovered like a satellite.

She was frail and slightly stooped and seemed dazed by all the people invading her home. Her gaze went longingly to the needlepoint frame as if it were her main means of sustenance. Ellen wondered if the demanding work made her life bearable, and she felt a surge of sympathy for the woman.

"I noticed the artwork on the pillows," she said gently. "Did you do all the needlepoint?"

The frail head bobbed. "She'd have the house covered in the stuff if she had her way," Little dismissed gruffly, leading them to the bar in the second living room. Without a word, the woman trailed after him, her eyes downcast.

Tom Gower and his wife left the group they were talking with to greet them. The deferential way the partners treated Kane proved his contention that money spoke.

Gower dismissed Ellen with cool disdain when Little introduced his daughter to Kane. Closer inspection reinforced her first impression. Florence Little Gower was a replica of her father, even to the vertical lines forming on her face. For the first time, she could almost understand Gower's need for someone else in his life.

Arthur and Lydia Bigelow were guests also, and his booming voice could be heard across the room. He was discussing the Tomas and Brown embezzlement scandal, and Ellen saw the two men wince. That topic was the last one desired by a room full of investors, and Gower hurried over to change the subject.

It brought to mind her negative thoughts about

145

Gower. Seeing him now, she knew she'd overreacted when she wondered if he might be following in Brown's footsteps. He liked his role in high finance too much to trade it for that of a thief. There were easier ways to compensate for what couldn't be changed, his young girl friend being one of them.

The room plan was typical of Victorian homes. The center hall divided the house, with the guest and family living rooms on either side. The dining room and kitchen were in the rear. When she went into dinner, Ellen saw that the fully extended mahogany table easily accommodated the two dozen guests. The damask tablecloth was a perfect background for the sparkling cut-glass goblets. The heirloom silver, heavy and ornate, dated from a time when a set for twenty-four was the accepted minimum in a bride's hope chest.

The catered meal went smoothly under Florence Gower's direction. Her mother was ignored, a pale ghost at her place at the foot of the table. As Ellen had anticipated, the solid period chairs were covered with examples of Olivia's exquisite needlepoint.

"Have you had enough?" Kane asked shortly after they finished their after-dinner drinks. "I'm ready to break out of here."

Ellen smiled teasingly at him. "You could have fooled me. You sounded quite interested in the conversation."

His eyelids lowered so that only she could see the lights glinting in his eyes. "I'm interested in many things. Right now my primary concern is seeing how fast I can peel you out of that dress you're wearing."

"Sex fiend," she breathed. "And you better unsizzle. Father and son-in-law are coming this way. They haven't missed that you're not letting me leave your side."

Kane's nostrils flared, and the lines bracketing his

mouth hardened. He hadn't forgotten his reaction when she related how Gower had come down hard on her. He'd also been aware of the speculation in Little's eyes whenever he saw them touch. Knowing it would accomplish nothing, he refrained from openly defying them by placing his arm around her as a warning that she was under his protection. Even more important, he knew the gesture would anger Ellen. About this set of circumstances, she was a very uptight lady.

"I'm sorry that we haven't had more time to be with you," Little apologized after Kane refused another brandy. His gaze drifted over Ellen, and he forced a lemony smile. "I see that Ms. Foster is doing her duty and seeing that your visit with us is without mishap."

Kane resented the man's attempt to find out what was going on between them, but he managed to clamp down on his temper. Anger on his part wouldn't help Ellen's tenuous position with them. "I must thank you for hiring her. I don't know much about New York, and she's been a wonderful help."

Little shifted under the steady stare that was successfully immobilizing him, and he gave a nervous laugh. "That sounds like a fine recommendation. Perhaps we'll take a closer look at Ms. Foster's contract."

"I would recommend her highly. I'm a very busy man, and coming to New York takes considerable planning. Although we use investment houses in Toronto, I like the way you do business. If you can guarantee that Foster Executive Services continues to be available to make my visits as pleasant as this, I'll make certain to come more often."

Little's back was to the wall, and he knew it. Kane's harsh gaze kept him pinned there, emphasizing his demand. He'd never squirmed before, but he felt the unpleasant sensation now.

Gower came to his partner's rescue. "Er, there are

147

several companies offering similar services, and we thought it only fair to check them all."

Kane's eyes stabbed him. "That's not good enough for me. By the way, I've been meaning to ask if you knew a good place to buy furs," he murmured smoothly.

Gower blanched. He pulled a sickly smile in place, conscious that his father-in-law was frowning at him in question at the odd change of topic. "I'm afraid my wife is the one with that information. Shall I ask her for you?"

"Tomorrow is Sunday, so the stores will be closed. It can wait until I see you Monday. Tell her that I'm especially interested in mink. I saw one the other day and thought it had possibilities."

Gower's hand trembled, causing the brandy in his glass to swirl in little eddies. "I'll see that I have the information for you," he finally managed to say.

"And it's settled about Ms. Foster's company?" Kane pressed.

Little reentered the conversation. Money was the one god he worshiped. It appeared that keeping Windsor an active client somehow depended on signing this woman's contract. If that was all it took, it was as good as done. There was still the cancellation clause in it that could be used later. For the moment, he'd do whatever it took to keep Windsor happy.

"Ms. Foster's contract will be in the mail on Monday," he promised with a small, pained smile.

"Fine," Kane answered. "And now I'm sorry to say we must leave. I have a busy day ahead of me tomorrow. Thank you for inviting us, and I hope both of you and your charming wives will be able to come to the party I'm having before I leave."

"Of course," Little assured him. "Olivia has it in her

148

appointment book already." Gower gulped down his brandy, and nervously nodded his agreement.

"Thank you for your help with my contract," Ellen said stiffly as they sped down the driveway minutes later. "Unfortunately, that clause about fraternization is still there to use as a club if they want to. After that pressuring you did, you don't think they haven't guessed what's between us, do you?" she asked bitterly.

"What's between us is strictly our business," he replied firmly. "As for clubs, we'll just have to make certain mine stays a little more threatening."

That was all well and good, Ellen thought bleakly. But once they had finished their business with Kane and he was safely back in Canada for another year, what protection could he be to her? How could she have let her hormones place her in this position? She'd been kissed by experts before and had been able to turn away from taking the final step. Why hadn't she had the will power with this man?

Because there were experts, and then experts, she had to admit. Kane's kisses affected her in a way no other man's ever had. They sizzled and they had burned away all thoughts of opposition before she'd been aware of what was happening.

Kane fought to keep his frustration from surfacing. He understood Ellen's reason for caution after the rumbles from Little and Gower. He'd spent a lifetime in the man-eat-man jungle of corporate business, and he knew all the games that were played. The cause for her concern had been removed by his using the power of money, the one threat he knew would be respected. Maybe his action had seemed ruthless to her and had precipitated the withdrawal that he now sensed in her.

The tires whined as they sped over the metal grid on the bridge. The sound cut into the silence that had settled between them. Ellen was inundated by guilt feelings by the time Kane pulled in front of her apartment. "No! I'm tired, and I want to sleep alone," she said when he slipped a folded bill to Bernie to take care of the car.

Kane ignored her, and she was made helpless again by her inability to create a scene as Bernie watched them walk to the elevator. She glowered as the elevator rose swiftly.

"I mean it," she repeated vehemently as she searched for her key when they reached her apartment.

He removed the evening bag from her hands and plucked out the missing object. "I'll have to buy you one of those large ornamental key chains so you don't have trouble locating your key like this all the time," he said indulgently, ushering her inside and closing the door behind them.

"Haven't you heard a word I said?" she demanded, refusing to go farther. Once he was in the living room, the battle would be half over. Her bedroom was just beyond, and its nearness was already triggering erotic memories that were weakening her hard-won resolve.

Kane examined her determined face. He'd been aware of her withdrawal on the way over, but he was not about to stand for it. Fantasies about what awaited him at the evening's end had made the intervening time bearable. "I heard you, all right. What I'd like to know is why you feel the need to erect a fence again. What we shared here last night was very special to me. I assumed it was the same to you?"

He didn't play fair! She fastened her gaze resolutely on the knot of his tie. It was a mistake. She remembered pressing her lips just inches above it onto the warm flesh. The sensation had been an aphrodisiac and had inspired her search for further areas to adore.

"You know it was," she stated firmly. "But that isn't the issue. It still was wrong, and succumbing to a moment's weakness doesn't excuse me. My company's reputation is still my primary concern."

Something snapped in Kane. He'd thought he'd put that problem behind them. The ache to hold her in his arms had been building all evening. Now the need seemed as necessary as breathing. Her obsession had to be eliminated once and for all. He had no desire to spend the night in a cold shower.

He grasped her shoulders and gave her a sharp shake. "Are you saying that what we felt was wrong? Do you really believe that what we shared can be casually dismissed as a moment's weakness?" he cried in amazement. "Maybe your memory needs a little readjusting to what actually occurred."

His mouth was on hers, hard and angry. Ellen gave a smothered protest. His kisses were the last thing she wanted. Verbal combat she could handle, but she knew her defenses quickly disintegrated under this kind of attack.

Having her in his arms at last, Kane's frustration disappeared and the harsh pressure eased. Now that she was where he wanted her, a strange tenderness enveloped him. No woman before had had the ability to arouse so many conflicting emotions in him. He wanted to shake sense into her, even while admiring her determination. Having been given glimpses of her vulnerability, he longed to protect her from harm. He championed her independence, even while vowing to tear down all fences where he was concerned.

The pressure she exerted against his shoulders slowly eased, and her body softened in that sweet undulation that was uniquely hers. With sweeping urgency, he molded her against him until every delicious curve blended into the planes of his body. His heart thudded heavily in his chest, and he felt the echoing beat throb through her. With no woman had he ever experienced this sense of oneness, this feeling that together they made a whole. For a moment the thought shook him. The sensation had begun the night before when they had climaxed together, but everything about their lovemaking had been shattering and he hadn't given it further thought.

The clothes preventing their complete joining were an abomination, but he had to make certain first that her defenses were demolished. When her mouth softened, permitting its exploration, he knew he was home free. His mouth, his hands, his body undulating against her gave explicit instructions to the emotions rioting in him. The possibility that she wasn't riding the crest with him was too incredible to contemplate. Never before had he been in such a state that even the hairs on his arms stood on end, giving painful pinpricks that demanded release from the incredible tension that had his body tied up in one huge ache. He'd have branded the phenomenon impossible if he weren't experiencing it himself.

He swung her up into his arms and carried her to her room. There their clothes were quickly removed as the impediments they were. They collapsed onto the bed to rediscover the magic that was theirs when they became one.

CHAPTER THIRTEEN

Ellen stared warily at Kane over her breakfast coffee. It was Monday, and the fantastic weekend was over. Within the hour she'd be immersed in the problems of running a business. Was that why the euphoria that had been hers all Sunday had evaporated?

The weekend had been wonderful, except for Kane's flexing of muscles at Little's party and her subsequent irritation. But his kisses had effectively wiped that reaction from her mind. Saturday night had held a touch of heaven, and Sunday had been nearly perfect. Neither had made a move without the other being by their side. Kane had even insisted she come along when he went to his hotel to get a change of clothes. That way he wouldn't have to leave her bed in the morning at the crack of dawn to get ready for an early appointment.

While they were there, Kane explained that the party he had mentioned at Little's was planned for Thursday. It was for cocktails and was to be held in his suite. He told her he usually gave one to help cement various business connections made during his visit.

He asked Ellen to handle the coordinating and she happily agreed. After all, it was one of the services her company performed for clients, she reminded him with an oblique smile.

Muscles bunched along his clenched jaw, and she

wondered what she'd said wrong. Then he told her he'd like her to act as his hostess. Realizing it would be the last thing she'd do for him before his return to Canada, she couldn't help but agree. Ellen was unprepared for the hollow ache that that realization brought with it.

The ache was with her again Monday morning as she sipped her coffee, and with it came the beginning of panic. Kane's departure wasn't supposed to cause pain. She certainly knew the rules of the game and was sophisticated enough to accept their relationship for the short-term affair that it had to be. He'd brought her to new and wonderful levels of passion, for which she should be grateful. If only the horrible doubt wasn't intruding that he was the only man who held the key to bringing her to those heights.

Another thought added to her wariness: How had he succeeded in tearing down her defenses? The realization of the depth of her vulnerability to his charms made her decidedly uncomfortable.

Playtime was over, Ellen knew. Why hadn't she been wise enough to follow her own rule against fraternization? She'd broken it, and now she had no one to blame but herself for her present distress. On Friday Kane would be out of her life. Hadn't he warned her in the beginning that his attention span was limited where women were concerned? In a month's time, he'd probably find it difficult to remember what she looked like. He'd certainly never recall his statement that what they had experienced together was special. A pain, as sharp as a scalpel, cut through her. In a reflex, she pressed her stomach to ease the ache. The shattering certainty came that no matter how quickly Kane forgot, no amount of time would be long enough to dull her memories.

"Have you made that appointment to see your doctor?" Kane demanded with a frown, seeing the telltale pressure being applied to her middle.

"Next week," Ellen lied glibly. She'd already diagnosed what caused these pains. Once he was gone and out of her life, she was certain the uncomfortable symptom would disappear.

Kane stared grimly at her as he ate the last of his toast. The bricks of the damn wall were being *mortared.* He'd assumed that he had shattered them completely, but evidently he'd only made a small hole. "I'll have Bella type the list of the people I asked to Thursday's party and get it to you. They've all been invited already, but perhaps you should check further with them."

"I'll put my staff on it. As soon as I get to the office, I'll call the hotel's kitchen about canapés and see that you have a well-stocked bar."

"Good," he commented with a small satisfied smile. She wasn't to know that Kane smiled because tonight he intended to have the pleasure of battering that wall down once and for all. He'd start with a kiss. When she was soft and melting, they'd talk and reach an understanding about some basic facts. Didn't she know by now that she could trust him not to hurt her, that there was no need for her to run in retreat?

"It's going to be a full day for me," he called as he went to the living room for his jacket. "I won't be able to pick you up at the office, but I'll meet you here about seven."

"I'm afraid I won't be here," Ellen called, keeping her head bent over the sink as she washed the dishes. She wasn't good at telling lies, and he'd proven all too often his ability to read her expressions. She heard him return to the kitchen, and she scrubbed the frying pan with careful attention.

155

"Where will you be?" he asked. His voice was carefully neutral.

"I didn't get to tell you, but my brother Philip is in town and I promised to see him after work." He was quiet so long that she gave a quick glance over her shoulder. His frown was black as he examined his watch.

He had a gut feeling that her story was a fabrication, but he didn't have the time to call her on it. Besides, with the mood she was in, telling her of his doubt wouldn't help matters. Good lord, hadn't yesterday been as outstanding for her as it had for him? A lot of matters needed discussing, he decided grimly.

"In that case, give me a call when you're back and I'll come then." Ignoring her soapy hands, he raised her chin with a finger and kissed her. "You've given me a very special weekend," he murmured. "I have no intention of letting it end there."

She locked the door behind him after he left, willing her incipient anger at the threat inherent in his words to grow. No man had jurisdiction over her life, and the sooner he realized it, the better.

Ellen welcomed the work waiting for her at the office. She knew she was running scared. That morning when she had looked at Kane's rugged features over the kitchen table, her emotional response to him fell into place. No ordinary man could have made her a traitor to a rule that was absolutely essential to the success of her company. But then, only a fool would consider Kane Windsor ordinary. The fact still remained that she'd done the unpardonable by consorting with a client.

Her mouth drooped in a parody of a smile. What an old-fashioned word *consort* was for something that was so new and beautiful. She sighed deeply as she accepted the fact that she'd done the unbelievable and

156

had actually fallen in love. She couldn't blame Kane for that. Not even during the fever of their lovemaking had he made any mention of that emotion. Oh, there'd been deliciously suggestive words that had stimulated reactions that still had her gasping, but love? Never, and only a fool would harbor hopes to ever hear them from him. Crazy she might be, but she was no fool.

Pure panic had driven her to fabricate a story about her brother as an excuse to avoid seeing him that evening. She'd played at being in love on a few occasions, but each time she'd known the truth for what it was. That morning's shock had been accompanied by the unshakable conviction that what she felt this time was the real emotion. Her first reaction had been to run and hide. No, she had to admit, the first was to dash into Kane's arms and to surprise him with the wonderful discovery before kissing him senseless.

That would have sent him scurrying for the hills, she told herself grimly. Somehow she'd remained rational and had gotten him out of the apartment. Making up the story about her brother was a smart move. Space was needed to come to grips with this crazy twist her life had taken. One thing was certain: Kane had to be kept at a distance so he wouldn't discover her foolish secret. When in his arms, she became disgustingly malleable, and it would be just like her to blurt out her discovery to him. How many hearts had he already captured? she wondered bleakly. Her pride demanded that he never know that hers had been added to the list.

She was eating a ham and Swiss sandwich with a decided lack of appetite when Jeanne sailed into her office. "I don't like to dance at someone's wake, but this should mean added business for us," she announced smugly.

Ellen looked at her cautiously. "Why do I have this feeling I might not agree with you?"

"I don't know why," Jeanne said airily. "I heard some interesting news. It's about Corporation Services, our new competitor. It seems two wives of clients assigned to them decided to spring a surprise visit on their husbands. You got it—two of their staffers were caught spending the night with them. One wife believed the bad press about the Big Apple and had come armed with a gun. Luckily, her aim wasn't very good, and only the mirror in the bedroom was shattered. With guns going off, the police got involved. Which meant it couldn't be hushed up. Boy, were we lucky to be able to hide that Peggy incident!

"It was their biggest contract, and I understand the company has now canceled out. We were talking about it just now, and we can understand more than ever why you're so emphatic about keeping our reputation clean."

Ellen's stomach lurched. Feeling slightly sick, she dropped the sandwich. Finding it impossible to meet her assistant's eyes, she reached for a pencil. Playing with it gave her something to focus on. "This can hurt us, too," she managed. "It's difficult enough to sell our services. This might ruin them, but we could find ourselves tarred with the same brush."

Jeanne's grin showed a blithe lack of concern. "Our reputation is so squeaky clean, we could pass for nuns. It's out in the marketplace that Little and Gower are our clients. Their narrow views on sex are the laugh of Wall Street, but the fact that they hired us is the best recommendation we could ask for."

Decidedly ill now, Ellen dismissed the subject with a wave of her hand and stated brusquely that she had more important things to attend to. She closed her mind to Jeanne's hurt look as she left the office. Later she'd attend to soothing her ruffled feelings. Now she had to cope with the overwhelming guilt brought on by her assistant's announcement.

What she had done was worse than what those women did. She'd set the rule, and she had broken it. She owned this company; it was her life and breath. How could she have forgotten her own fury when she found out that Peggy had stepped out of line, and her agonizing apprehension during the following months, wondering if the incident had leaked out and ruined her forever? How could she have done the unforgivable? And not only once; for several days, all her principles had been discarded because of the lure of being in a man's arms.

That being with Kane had been time spent out of this world, a gift with no comparison, was beside the point. For five long years, the dream of starting this company had been behind every move she'd made. Her success was the result of pure dedication and hard labor. What had happened at Corporation Services could be a death blow to them. If either Little or Gower should ever decide to call Kane's bluff, everything she'd slaved for would be less than dust.

By four o'clock Ellen had ended her self-flagellation, and she left the office with her resolution firmly in place. Her love remained unaltered, but she'd put it behind her. There would be no chance for it to grow anyway. Her shoulders shifted as if adjusting to the weight of her subsequent desolation. *Given time, this too will pass,* she promised herself grimly.

When she reached her apartment, her one desire was to curl up in bed and sleep the night away. She was limp with exhaustion, and it was more than just from not getting much sleep over the weekend. She gazed longingly at the bed, but she knew it wasn't for her. Kane was so persistent, he might actually check with

Bernie to make sure she had left to meet her brother. She was in no condition to discover what his reaction would be when he found out she was home alone. And even more important, her exhaustion had weakened her defenses. One touch of his hand, one kiss, and all the glorious memories would surface, making a shambles of any resolution she might be struggling to hide behind.

Accepting that the wisest course was flight, Ellen called an old college friend who'd become a professor and who had been after her to come for a visit. Amy was happy to hear from her and urged her to come right over. The more the merrier—a few friends had dropped by, and she knew she'd enjoy meeting them.

Bernie got her a taxi, and she was deposited half an hour later on Morningside Drive near Columbia University, where many of the faculty lived.

Amy welcomed her with open arms. After being introduced to the half-dozen people draped on the chairs and floor, Ellen sank onto the couch next to a bearded professor. He'd just returned from Spain and had brought to the party a *bota* full of a native red wine. With a flourish that brought cheers from the others over his expertise at handling the skin, he filled a glass for her.

The wine had a pleasant roughness that went well with the goat cheese that was also being served. Her tension gradually eased after the second glass. A pleasant relaxation came after the third. It wasn't until the fourth that Ellen remembered that she hadn't eaten since breakfast. The time with Kane had moved into the fuzzy past. It was enough that there was no more pain associated with him. In fact, it was pleasant to discover that thoughts of the future were encased in the same fuzzy haze as was the present. Hours later, she waved a limp hand good-bye to the kind professor when he left with the empty goatskin under his arm.

"Feeling better?" Amy asked kindly, fluffing a pillow behind Ellen's head.

The room shifted alarmingly, but it felt good to stretch out on the couch. "More than better. S'feel great," she slurred.

Amy nodded wisely. "And tomorrow will be hell, but we won't talk about that now. Good friend that I am, I won't even ask if something happened at your company or if it was a man who sent you scurrying here. When you're feeling better, I expect a full report."

Ellen blinked owlishly, marveling over her friend's astuteness. She offered no resistance when her sandals were removed and the fastenings undone on her jeans.

"I could pour you into a taxi, but I doubt you're in any condition to get yourself to bed," Amy continued amiably, drawing a light blanket over her. "You're lucky tonight. The couch is free, so you can use it."

Amy turned off the lights, and Ellen curled into a ball. "Oh, Kane!" she whispered before exhaustion overtook her.

Hearing Ellen's half-sob, Amy paused at the door and nodded understandingly. It was a man, just as she suspected. Her business caused a lot of problems, but Ellen always met those challenges. Only a man could have brought her to Amy's door looking like a lost waif.

Ellen groaned when she felt someone shake her shoulder, and she pressed her hands to her temples to stop the sound from crashing through her head.

"I hate waking you, but I have a class this morning, and I didn't know if you have to be at your office."

Ellen managed to open one eye a fraction. "Lord yes, but oh, what happened to me?" she whispered. Her head felt as if it were about to explode.

"Wine tends to do that," Amy replied with cheerful callousness. "Here, drink this seltzer. It's the best I can do. Unless you want coffee? No, I didn't think so," she admitted quickly, seeing her friend gag. "Come on, drink up, and then it's into the shower for you."

Ellen managed to raise herself and wondered if this was how a zombie felt. After some consideration, she decided it wasn't. The lucky things weren't supposed to have any feelings at all. She somehow managed to down the seltzer, and with Amy's assistance, she removed her clothes and managed to reach the bathroom.

"How do the Spaniards survive drinking that stuff?" Ellen groaned later. Her arms were braced on the kitchen table as she stared balefully at a cup of black coffee.

"I don't think they drink six glasses of wine in two hours on an empty stomach—and it was empty, wasn't it?" Amy asked knowingly. "As I recall, you have a habit of forgetting to eat when you're under pressure."

"You must have been listening to Kane," Ellen muttered. Seeing her friend's eyes brighten with interest, she took a sip of coffee. "Thanks for putting me up, but I have an appointment that can't be put off, and you did say you had a class."

Ellen walked into her office on shaky legs an hour later. She'd stopped off at her apartment to change her clothes, and she was thankful that Bernie wasn't on duty. It was best not to know if Kane had tried to contact her or what his mood had been if he had.

"It must have been some night," Jeanne commented drily after giving her report on a client who had flown in and out the day before.

"Don't ever drink wine from a *bota*," Ellen replied darkly, reaching for the ringing phone. "It has a nasty way of sneaking up on you."

"What does?" Anger underlined the question, which was asked by the voice on the phone.

Ellen caught her breath. Just hearing him, she knew that the wine hadn't solved anything. The smart move would have been to remain home and unplug the phone.

"Hello, Kane. The list of names arrived, and I'm waiting for a final report on which people will actually be coming. We called the chef at the hotel, and I think you'll like the selection of hors d'oeuvres he recommended. I also saw that a qualified bartender will take care of the drinks, and I hired a woman to pass out the food and see to the ashtrays and empty glasses."

Kane listened to the cool control in her voice and frowned. Was someone there with her? He didn't care. The night before, he'd phoned every hour from ten to three and had even demeaned himself by checking with the security guard and asking to be notified no matter what time she returned. He'd even called her apartment twice that morning. It was possible that a woman stayed out overnight with her brother, he tried to tell himself. Possible, but not probable. He had every intention of finding out what type of game she thought she was playing. He'd never done this kind of checking with any woman, and he was angry that he felt he had to do it now.

"I'm leaving the details to you," he said dismissively. "Where in the world were you last night? You said you'd call when you got home, and I waited until after midnight." He wasn't about to tell her he'd worn his finger off to a nub dialing her number.

"I'm sorry, Kane. I guess we just lost track of time, what with catching up on family gossip." Thank goodness he wasn't here seeing her squirm in the chair. What was it about this man that made her squirm every time she didn't tell the truth?

"Will I see you tonight?"

She flinched at his terse question. *Yes,* every part of her wanted to cry, but she compressed her lips and inhaled deeply. "He's leaving in the morning, so I promised to spend the evening with him again."

The silence extended until she thought he'd hung up. "I'm coming at one and taking you to lunch. Be ready." The phone clicked in her ear. His order was explicit. He wasn't permitting any evasion.

Perhaps this was best, Ellen consoled herself. In a public place like a restaurant, he'd be unable to touch or kiss her. A man was vulnerable where his pride was concerned, and she'd hit him there. She'd explain in words of one syllable that what they'd had was over, finished, done.

Ellen waited for Kane's arrival with relative calm. At least her love would remain her secret.

CHAPTER FOURTEEN

Ellen smiled her thanks as Miles Walker raised his glass in a toast. "To a gracious hostess. I guarantee that if my business ever grows enough to be able to afford you, I intend to be a client."

She smiled graciously. "I'm glad Kane was able to solve your packaging problems." It seemed aeons since they'd met on the terrace at Bigelow's party. "And as for hiring my company, I'm going to hold you to that."

After making sure his glass was full, she introduced him to a man who she recalled was involved with color imprints. They were soon deep in conversation about problems with dye casting on various papers, and she moved on to make certain that the rest of the guests were having a good time.

Miles was right, she admitted with pride as her gaze swept the room. Everyone appeared to be relaxed and enjoying themselves. She was particularly pleased with the changes that had been made in the suite. The tall greens the florist had placed in the corners softened the impersonal look of the hotel room. To allow more room for the guests, she had had the bar set up in the guest room, with screens hiding the bed.

She'd arrived early to check that all was ready. When Kane had opened the door to her knock, his black eyes had become almost incandescent. The lights eased some of the ache that wouldn't go away.

Ellen had bought a dress especially for the occasion. The white silk crepe was cut in Grecian lines, leaving one golden shoulder bare. A complicated French twist brought attention to the rich texture of her hair. Her slender neck was accented by long gold chains that dangled from her ears. She wanted Kane to remember her looking her best.

She pressed a finger against her temple to ease the throbbing. The ache had been with her ever since their lunch date. Aspirins didn't help, so she resigned herself to its discomfort, certain that it would disappear when he was back in Canada—tomorrow.

With a quick glance, she made sure that none of the guests, held an empty glass, then her mind drifted back to that disastrous meeting. There was no reason to call it that; the results had been exactly what she wanted. She'd arrived at the restaurant armed with her determination. Before he could question her about her fictitious evening with her brother, she'd launched into her speech.

Kane had listened quietly to her reasons why what they shared had to end. His only reaction had been the grim set to his lips. When she finished, he'd stared at her with cold speculation. "So that's that, then," he'd said noncommittally, and changed the subject.

There'd been no arguments, no attempt to manipulate. Ellen felt strangely bereft and blamed it on the fact that she'd braced herself to fight any rebuttal he might make. His dismissal proved what she had long suspected, that she had been a pleasant interlude but hardly worth fighting for. He'd only have to smile that smile of his, to kiss that damnable kiss of his, and he'd have a replacement. They had barely touched their lunch, and they'd parted with a cordial good-bye. The following days, all messages had gone through Bella.

She hadn't seen or heard from him again until he opened the door that evening. He was still in his shirt, and he was working gold links into the cuffs. Images of another time, when she'd lain in bed admiring his long fingers performing that same chore, flashed through her mind. Memories shouldn't hurt like that!

On entering the room, Ellen quickly shifted her gaze away from him but not before catching that flare of hungry desire that could melt bones. When she had the courage to glance at him again, it was gone, and she wondered if her need to see if he held any memories had made her imagine it.

The Littles arrived, followed by the Gowers, and any reservations the two men might have had about what was between them seemed to have been satisfied. Kane was the perfect host, and his attitude toward her was pleasant but cool.

She pressed harder at her throbbing temple and wished away the dull pain that lay like a lead weight deep within her. The evening was bound to end soon, and she'd be free of the torture of seeing him at every turn and knowing he was beyond reach. Anticipating a difficult evening, she thought she was armed. The weakness that permeated her when she saw him again proved to her how pitiful her preparations were. Tasting the potency of his virile masculinity hadn't created an immunity to it. It had, if anything, intensified her sensitivity to him.

"Headache?" The deep voice questioned from behind her.

Ellen turned slightly to see him better. "A slight one. I'm hoping that if I ignore it, it will go away."

Kane's dark eyes searched her face. "Those shadows weren't under your eyes before. Have you seen that doctor yet? In addition to not eating correctly, I bet you're not getting enough sleep."

Her thin smile was mocking. He was, of course, right on both counts. "Still checking on me, Dr. Windsor? Aren't you lucky you're leaving tomorrow and can drop this concern about my habits!"

His bleak look was replaced by a harsh smile. "You told me very clearly that you couldn't care less about how I feel."

He turned abruptly and joined several guests on the other side of the room, leaving Ellen lost in misery that seemed to have no ending. That glimpse of his pain was a revelation. He was a man of pride, and she'd hurt him in ways she was only now beginning to understand. He'd given her his protection, something she was certain he extended to few people. He'd given her affection that was exquisite in its savage tenderness. It wasn't his fault that she'd fallen in love and wanted more. In reaction, she'd panicked like some inexperienced teen-ager and slammed the door in his face rather than coping on a rational level.

Instead of enjoying the gift of what he gave her, she rejected it and had suffered as a result. How often was she going to act like a fool before wisdom came? He was so right in saying that what they shared was unique. Hadn't the agonizing emptiness of the past few days shown her just how special their relationship had been?

True, her company policy was necessary, but no rule was unbreakable. Compared to the knowledge that tomorrow Kane would be gone forever, it had no meaning.

Suddenly, all sham dropped away. Ellen admitted to herself the reason she had dressed so seductively, admitted to her childish desire to taunt Kane over what he'd lost. But beyond that, she'd hoped that his desire would be so overpowering that he'd batter down her defenses so that afterward she could blame this last night together on the fact that he'd seduced her.

She didn't like what she had discovered about herself. And now honesty demanded that she admit to what she desired: one last night with Kane, a night that would have to nourish her until time faded the temper of her love.

She soon discovered that acknowledging her desire and realizing it were two very different questions. From his cool attitude tonight, she knew that Kane had accepted her ultimatum. Now she wondered if there were enough sparks remaining in the ashes of what they had had to be fanned into flames. All she could do was try. This last night she intended to give Kane her love.

After Ellen made her decision, the throbbing at her temples, the leaden weight, disappeared. A glow radiated from her, adding luster to her eyes. Her body flowed with a pulsing rhythm, turning her walk into a melody of sinuous grace.

It wasn't long before she knew dark eyes were following her lithe movements. She flashed seductive smiles and noticed indulgently the taut slash of his mouth. If he thought she was teasing him, he was right. Later, she hoped he'd recognize her performance as a subtle foreplay for things to come.

"You should consider getting married," Kane said after good-byes were exchanged with the last departing guest. "Your hostessing ability would be a plus for some lucky man who was ambitious to climb the corporate ladder."

Ellen arched a brow at him. "I'd prefer that he had other reasons for marriage."

His smile was enigmatic. "I'm sure any man would be able to think of many other reasons."

"I better check to see how the cleaning is progressing." Her voice sounded strangled. Where was her decision to seduce this man now that everyone was gone?

"They're paid to know their job. Relax and have a final drink with me. It was interesting to see how you made one cocktail last the evening."

Something heated deep within her. Had he really been keeping that close an eye on her? "You had very little yourself. I noticed only one refill."

His smile let her know she'd given herself away. "I'm not a host who tries to outdrink his guests. Besides, I had other concerns on my mind."

"Oh? Some unfinished business?" she asked as he handed her a martini and she sank into the velvet sofa. He joined her there, much to her satisfaction.

He stared at his drink before looking at her with a self-mocking expression. "You could call it that. I was wondering when the breaking point would come, and I'd end up crushing Miles Walker's hand if he didn't stop touching you."

Ellen gasped in surprise. True, Miles had been with her often during the evening, but she'd accepted that it was because he knew so few of the guests. As a result, she'd played the proper hostess and introduced him around. She had no recollection of him touching her. Her concentration had been centered on the dark-haired man around whom the room was now pivoting.

Kane's attention focused on her softly pursed lips. With a muffled exclamation, he took her drink from her and deposited it on the table. His fingers were cool from the glass as they held her chin. Then he made her aware of the power of his hunger.

Kane kissed her fiercely, as if driven by a need to reacquaint himself with each delicious angle of her mouth. He was angry now, angry that this woman still affected him so profoundly, even though he'd decided that their affair was over. When she'd sat so primly opposite him in that damn restaurant, he'd wanted to shove the table aside and sweep her in his arms, where he knew his kisses would silence her silly rejections. But he'd been halted by the glimpse of her vulnerability and, most damnably, her fear. That she thought there was reason to fear him caused him to hesitate. Then pride and frustration had made him angry, and he had let her walk out of his life.

That evening when he opened the door at her knock, it had taken only one look, and he knew that the final chapter on what was between them hadn't been written as yet. Their eyes had met, and he'd felt her response before her mask slipped in place. She was politely cool, and he found himself watching her carefully, searching for a crack. Then, as if wishes could be made to come true, her attitude did an about-face halfway through the party. He swore the signals were for him until he noticed that miserable Walker acting possessively of her.

But she was in his arms now, and she was melting in that delightful way of hers that always did exciting things to him. Exultation rose in him at the knowledge that this night would be his. Nothing, he vowed, would come between him, this woman, and the heaven to which she so easily transported him.

One part of his mind heard the soft click of the door, alerting him that the helpers had gone. Ellen's mouth opened under his, and his attention focused on the immediacy of what that soft parting did to his libido.

He moaned his desire, and Ellen responded with an instinct older than time. Her body softened and conformed to please this sleek animal, to invite him to

171

share in that ultimate rite for the continuation of the species.

How perfectly her mouth and her tongue were formed for seduction, she marveled as a tremor rippled through him. The small pearl studs on his formal shirt parted under her fingers as they searched for the warm flesh hidden behind the fine linen.

Their breaths were ragged when he finally released her mouth. "I think we'd better go to my room," he suggested in a gravelly voice. They reached his bed, and he shook his head in frustration when he found he was unable to locate the zipper to her dress. "You better remove that before it gets torn," he warned.

Ellen released the hidden closures and slipped the dress over her head. Her hose and lacy bikini followed. She turned and found Kane had shed his clothes also. Though she'd seen him nude before, the beauty of his male body still had the power to stun her, and her avid examination showed her pleasure.

"Come," he said gruffly. She stepped closer, and with slow deliberation he removed the hairpins, letting them drop to the carpet. Her hair fell over her shoulders, and he filled his hands with the silken strands. Burying his face in the soft mass, he breathed deeply of the beguiling scent and realized that he still hadn't discovered the name of the perfume she used.

He followed her into the bed and gathered her close. His arms had been empty too long. All of him had been empty too long, he corrected while fighting the need to take her in one explosive release. In twenty-four hours he'd be gone, and the chances of having her again in his bed were slim. He intended to make these remaining hours special and brand them in her memory forever.

She moaned softly, savoring his flesh, warm and

damp to her touch. They remembered with unerring accuracy all the areas that brought him pleasure.

"You're a she-devil," he accused huskily as he braced his elbows on each side of her so he could admire the way her hair cascaded over the pillow.

Ellen gazed at him with eyes heavy with desire. Passion gave color to his body and flushed his cheeks. His eyes had the hard shine of anthracite coal. They bored into her as if searching for her soul. For one heartbeat, she almost bared it and told of her love, but he bent his head and took her mouth, drawing deep of its essence before giving equal attention to the hard buds his experienced fingers created on the crests of her breasts.

She breathed deeply of his evocative scent and knew the aroma would haunt her forever. Finally, when kisses weren't enough, when touching brought the fires to their highest flames, they joined to become one.

A shift in the mattress awakened Ellen from a deep sleep. She stretched with lazy grace as a smile of deep contentment played on her lips.

"I hate to wake you, princess," Kane confessed ruefully, "but my plane leaves in three hours, and I don't think you'll want to be found here by the maid."

She sat up with a start. Kane pressed a quick kiss onto her lips before reaching for a clean shirt. She absorbed the pure maleness of the man clad only in black knit briefs, and she wept silently.

Her last night was over, she realized with numb acceptance. Their lovemaking had been more than special. The second time had been a frenzy, as if they were driven by the fact their night would soon be over. But by dawn their love held a gentleness that brought tears to her eyes. She poured all her love into the

173

tender exchange, love that could be expressed no other way.

"Breakfast will soon be here, but you have time for a quick shower," he informed her.

"I won't take long," Ellen promised. Each additional minute with him was an extra gift that she accepted gratefully.

Ellen returned to the bedroom, a towel her only cover. Her expression clouded in dismay when she examined her party gown. "Now I'm going to find out how you men feel when you have to leave the morning after. No way can I pretend this dress is meant for day wear."

Seeing her embarrassment, Kane reached quietly for the phone. Ten minutes later a box bearing the imprint of the dress shop in the hotel lobby arrived.

"I hope it fits," he said, handing her the box. "I'm afraid I couldn't do anything about shoes, but in New York I doubt anyone will think it's odd that they're gold."

"Thank you," Ellen whispered over the lump in her throat. His sensitivity to her feelings shook the already-precarious hold she had on her emotions. The shirtwaist dress was pale blue; the basic design was made chic by a peacock blue sash. By the time she was dressed, breakfast arrived. Then the message came that Ralph was waiting with the limousine, and Kane asked for a bellhop to come for his cases.

"I don't want you to come with me," Kane ordered firmly. "I hate prolonged good-byes." His kiss was bruising in its intensity, but Ellen felt only the anguish of the parting. "Remember me, princess," he said roughly as a knock sounded at the door. "And remember how special what we shared was."

He was gone then, and Ellen was left with the crumbs on the tray, a rumpled bed, and the remnants of a dream that had never had a chance.

CHAPTER FIFTEEN

Jeanne examined her boss critically and shook her head. "Pardon the bluntness, but you look like something even a cat wouldn't want to drag in. After your successful trip to Atlanta and Dallas, I would have thought you'd be on top of the world. I hear the reports for the first month show that both offices have already turned in a profit. That's cause for a celebration, which is why I'm here. Let's go someplace expensive tonight and order a bottle of champagne. With Foster Executive Services picking up the check, of course."

Ellen leaned back in her chair, a faint smile easing the lines of fatigue on her face. "That sounds like one of your better ideas. What expensive place do you have in mind?"

"Top of the Sixes?" Jeanne suggested with a roguish smile. "I love looking down on the Manhattan skyline when I'm eating. It gives me a feeling of power."

"Fine, and speaking of power, I want to compliment you again on how well you ran this office while I was gone."

Jeanne shrugged her slender shoulders. "There weren't any horrendous problems. It practically ran itself."

"I'm thinking of opening a branch in Chicago. Are you certain I can't persuade you to head it?"

"No way!" Her refusal was emphatic. "Some people might be able to exist outside of New York, but not me. By the way, remember Frances Agee, Kane Windsor's secretary who ended up in the hospital because of her allergy to shrimp? She called twice while you were away, and she wants you to call her as soon as you can."

She left the office after giving the information and didn't notice that the color drained from her boss's face. Ellen sat with her eyes closed as despair washed over her. It was unfair that after all she had done these past two months to eradicate Kane's memory from her mind, a casual mention of his name could still do this to her.

The memory of that day two months before when he'd left flooded back. He hadn't even said anything about meeting her again. It had taken a few days before she had accepted that a clean break was best. It would have been worse waiting for what wasn't because of an empty promise.

Luckily, the following weeks had been busy. With the contract with Little and Gower safely signed, she immersed herself in the work involved in getting her satellite branches going. Their other clients kept her staff working to their limit. Ellen sighed. Yes, there was cause to celebrate. If only it weren't such an effort to dredge up the enthusiasm.

She could keep her days filled. It was the nights that drained her. Thoughts of Kane persisted in haunting her until she seriously thought about getting rid of the bed where they'd slept together. But then the sofa where he had sprawled would have to go also, and the kitchen table where they had shared breakfast.

Jeanne had no idea how welcomed her suggestion

was. Ellen would make certain the dinner was a leisurely one, and with the aid of the champagne perhaps she'd get a good night's sleep for a change.

When she was certain her control was in place, she asked Bella to call Toronto. Over the past month, she'd talked to Frances several times. The woman had persisted in doing the preliminary work in preparation for opening her escort service. She dreaded the calls since Kane's name usually crept into the conversation. But during their last conversation, the woman stated that a replacement had been found, and she was training her to Kane's way of working. She was looking forward to being free and was eager to concentrate on opening her own business.

"Thank you for calling," Frances said when Bella opened the line. "I've got disturbing news, and I don't know how to tell you."

Ellen's knuckles whitened. Dear Lord, had something happened to Kane? "What is it?" She was surprised she could speak, far less breathe.

"Bob—that's my husband—found out that his company is transferring him to San Francisco. I'm absolutely devastated. I've put so much research time into this, and I was ready to move. I even found a perfect office site and was about to sign a lease. Now it's all wasted," she moaned. "I've never come this close to thinking divorce, and if I didn't love the big lug, I would. I want this so bad, I can taste it!"

Ellen could relate to Frances's dismay. On the strength of the woman's enthusiasm, she had been planning new letterheads stating that her company was international. Her lips twisted in a wry grimace. The best-laid plans of mice and men . . .

"How terrible for you!" she sympathized. "But the move needn't be the end of your dream. You've learned how to do the necessary research, and once you're settled in San Francisco, there's no reason you can't open an office there."

Frances thought about that idea for a minute. "Do you really think so?" she asked with rising interest.

"Of course. San Francisco is considerably larger than Toronto and should give you even more scope. In fact, when you got me thinking about franchises, I had surveys done in various cities and San Francisco was one of them. I'll send you the results."

"Mr. Windsor told me not to be disappointed, that something better was certain to come along, but I was too crushed to believe it."

The old familiar pain started in her stomach. "How is Mr. Windsor?" The question slipped out before she realized it.

"He's been working even harder than usual. I believe he told you that Windsor Cardboard is one of his special companies. They've been having a lot of trouble, and he's been practically living at the plant.

"He'll be happy to hear your solution to my problem. You know it's partly because of his interest and suggestions that I got so much research done. He was very impressed with your company and always asks how you are when he hears we've talked. I'm sure he'd send his regards if he knew I was talking to you."

I'm certain he would too. Unfortunately, what I want is more involved than his regards. But at least so far he hadn't forgotten her. The thought held little consolation when she wanted so much more.

Ellen hung up the phone and stared out the window in helpless resignation. In spite of her work to bring it to an end, her love hadn't dissipated one iota. Her heart thudded just as hard on hearing those scraps of information that she hungered for as it did when she was lying in his arms, with him surging above her.

She rubbed the tense muscles along her neck with a

weary gesture. Jeanne was right—she looked awful. Her sleepless nights and her lack of appetite were taking their toll. She glanced at her calendar. She'd had ten days with Kane; one would think two months would be long enough to get over him. It had been summer, and it was now fall. If she were lucky she'd have this sickness licked by Christmas.

"Celebrations are a vile form of torture," Ellen grumbled when she reached the office. She tore open the silver packet and watched with jaundiced eyes as the two tablets dropped into the water and filled the glass with a stream of bubbles. Perhaps she and Jeanne had gone into it with too much enthusiasm, she admitted morosely. Anyone with sense knew that two margaritas followed by a bottle of champagne showed lack of wisdom. Then they'd stopped in the lounge, and not wanting to give up her relaxed state, she had attempted to prolong it with vodka martinis. She hadn't seen Jeanne yet. No doubt she was in her office huddled over a glass of her own cure-all.

"Mr. Gower is on line two," Bella announced through the intercom.

Ellen grimaced and quickly drained the salty mixture before reaching for the phone. One of these days, she supposed, she'd come to terms with her dislike for that man and would be able to feel more at ease when dealing with him. Ever since Kane's ultimatum, she couldn't fault Gower's treatment, but having been exposed to the other, ugly side of him, she was constantly on the alert for its return.

"I have good news for you, but I bet you already know what it is." He greeted her with a brittle laugh that put her immediately on guard.

"I'm afraid you'll have to tell me, Mr. Gower," she

said coolly. "If it's good news, I definitely want to hear it."

He hesitated as if choosing the right words. "We just received an unexpected call. A client is on his way, and we want you to pick him up at noon."

Ellen did some rapid calculations in her mind. A customer's plane was leaving out of Newark International, but Ralph should be back from New Jersey with the limousine by then. "Certainly. I'll have one of my staff there to greet him. I need the name of the airline he's coming in on and his name. Has he made arrangements with a hotel for his stay?"

Gower's voice tightened oddly. "No, no, he was most adamant that *you* be the one to greet him."

The telltale ache gripped her middle, and she knew the answer before she even asked the question. "I'm afraid I didn't get the name of your client."

"Didn't I say?" he asked. He laughed again, this time very nervously. "It's Kane Windsor from Toronto."

It's physically impossible for one's heart to stop and still live, Ellen assured herself. It was possible, however, to protect it from further pain. "I'm afraid my schedule is too tight to accommodate him. I'll have my assistant do the honors."

Gower was now in command and his voice tightened. "I'm afraid I didn't make myself clear, Ms. Foster. Mr. Windsor is adamant that *you* be the one to meet him. I have no intention of losing him as a client because you have scheduling problems."

The pressure Kane applied must have been formidable, but why? Her question persisted as she took down pertinent information about his arrival. It followed her as Ralph steered the sleek limousine through the busy streets. Traffic was worse than usual,

180

and they arrived at LaGuardia minutes before the plane landed.

There'd been little time for Ellen to come to grips with the turmoil that Gower's message had brought on. She had even less time to adjust to the idea that in seconds Kane would once again be in her life.

He came through the arrival gate with his long, assured stride. The mending of her heart had been based on the belief that she'd never see him again. With one ripping pull, all the fine stitches were torn out, exposing gaping holes that she had no time to patch.

His dark eyes swept the waiting crowd to find her. Neither of them smiled as he came to her, his gaze fastened on her face. "Hello, princess," he said quietly.

Ellen quivered in response to the husky way he always spoke that special name. His eyes were telling her he remembered when he had whispered it in her ear in the dark of the night.

Someone rushed forward and jostled Ellen; it was enough to bring her out of her stunned state. Good lord, she thought in disgust, did he think he could walk out of her life and then just walk back in? Surely her pride and self-esteem rated better than that!

"It's good to see you again, Kane," she managed with a cool nod. "Did you bring much luggage with you?"

His lashes lowered as he examined her. "Just what I have with me," he said. He carried a soft suit bag over his back.

"You're traveling light. I take it you're not staying long this time."

"I hope not, but I'll stay as long as it's necessary to finish what has to be done."

Her smile was bright and utterly false. "Then I'll

wish you success. I can understand how precious your time is."

A frown creased Kane's brow as he took her elbow and led her from the airport. He must have been dreaming if he thought she'd fall into his arms when seeing him. Maybe he should have packed more than one suit. His jaw jutted in determination. He'd buy a dozen suits if that was how long it took to swing her to his way of thinking.

"It's not that my time is precious. It's just that I keep running out of it," he explained once the limo had pulled away from the busy terminal.

Ellen wasn't interested in how he'd spent the months since she'd last seen him. She simply accepted that there'd been a replacement for her. She pressed her middle, then swore to herself when she saw that he had noticed the movement. Those stomach pains had ended with his departure and had only returned after Gower's call a few hours ago.

"How is Frances Agee?" she asked quickly before he could question her about doctor appointments that never took place. "It's too bad about her husband's transfer coming just when she was ready to start her own company."

"I look at it differently. What if she'd sunk her money into it, and he was transferred before she could build it to where she could make a profit by selling it?"

"You've got a point there," she admitted. "Still, it's too bad that all her work is for nothing."

Kane shifted slightly so he had a better view of her profile. His plan had seemed so simple before, but now that he was with this vibrant woman, he wondered if his ability to manipulate would be enough.

"You're right, it would be a shame. I know how hard she worked. Have you ever thought of buying the files from her and opening the office yourself?"

182

Her eyes widened at the suggestion, and he smiled, seeing the idea take hold. It had happened often enough to him, and he enjoyed watching her weigh the pros and cons in quick succession. He always admired the professional part of her. It was when the other facets of her interesting personality began to hold his attention that he managed to get in trouble. Deep trouble.

"That has interesting possibilities," she admitted thoughtfully.

"I figured that would appeal to you," he agreed. Maybe he'd get her to Canada yet. As the past two months had proved, the miles that separated them were a definite barrier. They had showed him how difficult it was to block enough free time to fly to New York.

Ralph drew up in front of the Plaza, and Ellen smiled politely as she made her little speech. "I understand your company handled the reservations. If there is anything further we can do to make your stay a pleasure, please let us know. The limousine will be at your service if you let us know when you're leaving."

His hand was on her arm, urging her out. "I want you to come with me so I can discuss my itinerary."

Alarm bells rang. *Oh, no you don't!* She'd gone that route once before, and look where it had landed her. No way was she going to go to his suite to do anything.

He closed his eyes for a moment, and she was surprised by the fatigue she saw in his face. "Don't make this difficult, Ellen. I've put in two hard months working under constant pressure. When I arrived in Toronto, I discovered that the factory we had just bought was on the brink of a strike. Then a forest fire wiped out some of our prime timber, severely burning two of our men in the process. And even worse, my mother had a heart attack and we almost lost her."

The pain in his face was her undoing. Every part of her ached to hold his weary head and ease away the lines with loving caresses. "How is your mother doing?" she asked softly as she stepped out of the car.

"The doctors released her from the coronary care unit yesterday, which is why I am able to be here today."

She followed him into the hotel, wondering what business deal made coming to New York so important. Once the groundwork was laid, any adjustments to a portfolio could be carried out over the phone.

One thing Ellen liked about the Plaza was that once you were a guest, your name was seldom forgotten. In what could appear to be a cold impersonal city, it was pleasant to be greeted by name even by the bell captain. After Kane signed the registration card they were whisked up to the same suite he had occupied before.

She sat primly on a velvet-cushioned chair until the bellboy deposited Kane's luggage in the closet and left. She kept her eyes averted from the bedroom: Too many memories lay in that room. It was also where a futile dream had died unborn.

"A drink?" he asked, opening the cabinet, which revealed a small refrigerator and bar setup.

Ellen shuddered, thinking of the evening's celebration that she was still paying for. "Nothing for me, thanks. But don't let that stop you. You did say something about an itinerary?" She had a strong feeling of *déjà vu*. He'd lured her to this room once before with that excuse, and she had never been the same from that day on. Her shoulders squared, and she clutched her purse on her lap as a shield. She was a quick learner. The first mistake can be blamed on lack of knowledge. Any after that resulted from pure stupidity.

Kane looked at the selection before deciding that a

drink could be lethal in his exhausted state. He needed all his wits around him to pull this off. This woman was not only sharply intelligent, she'd been hurt and therefore was doubly on the defensive.

He dropped onto the sofa and searched for a crack in her careful control. He swore softly. He should have followed his inclination at the airport and taken her in his arms when he first saw her. He wouldn't have to try to knock those walls down once again now.

"I wasn't looking for sympathy before when I told you about the load I've been carrying. It was a partial explanation of why you haven't heard from me the past two months."

Ellen met his gaze steadily. "I never expected anything more. There's no reason to apologize."

He winced before raking his fingers through his hair. "That's what I kept telling myself. I was home only two days, and I knew that line had nothing to do with the facts. The truth is that what we had was special, and I was a fool to think I could walk away from it." His mouth twisted in a wry smile in recognition of his stupidity.

"I spent all too much time devising methods of luring you to Toronto, and more specifically to my bed. Then the walls caved in. My pride got in the way when my father said to let the fools go on strike and close down the plant. He said we would be ahead by using it as a tax writeoff. But I'd worked too hard to get the Board to buy it, and I felt my integrity was on the line. I've been sweating through around-the-clock meetings to work out a contract that we could all live with. Then there was the fire—and my mother."

His eyes closed, and his head dropped back to rest on the sofa. He looked drained, and Ellen again fought the need to wipe away the weariness with tender kisses and soothing fingertips.

185

"And all through the mess, I was haunted by the fact that time was slipping away, and with each day that passed the chances of us getting back together were less and less."

"There was the telephone," she reminded him bitterly, recalling the nights she'd spent staring at the instrument, willing it to ring with a long-distance call, even though she knew it never would.

His head remained back, but his eyes opened in slits so he could look at her. "Would you have dropped everything and come?" he asked in a mocking voice. "Your business is as important to you as mine is to me. The logistics of the distance separating us were defeating me, and I was too exhausted to work out how it could be handled."

"You mean you're suggesting a long-distance affair?" If that was all she could have, would it be enough? It startled her that she was actually giving it thought.

He looked at her strangely as if suddenly seeing her with a new clarity. He rose and went to the window to stare across the road at the fall colors tinting Central Park. Then he turned back to her. "That was my original intention," he admitted in dawning wonder. "But I just realized what a blind fool I've been. My God, I should have suspected what was happening when I pressured you the way I did. I've never worked so hard before to get a woman into my bed. Nor did I ever have the urge to demolish someone before because he was paying that woman extra attention. And as for Gower's attempt at blackmail—"

He shook his head in disbelief at his denseness. "You had me acting like a knight riding into battle to protect you, and I never recognized how out of character that was for me."

This time her hand was pressed to her breast. Her

heart was thudding as if it wanted to escape. Was it possible she was interpreting his words correctly.

"The real reason I was rushing here to present my case to you never occurred to me. When Frances spoke about all her research going to waste, it came to me that if you had a branch in my city, it would give us a reason to see more of each other. But now—" He paused as if uncertain, and his eyes exposed a sudden doubt. "Ellen, will you consider ruling your empire from Toronto?"

"Why?" she whispered. Was it possible that dreams really did come true?

"Because I love you, and I want you to marry me."

"Kane, what took you so long?" She was out of the chair and in his arms where she belonged. She thrived on challenges, and for a few seconds her mind buzzed with the adjusting that needed to be done. With the knowledge already hers, starting a new business would be a piece of cake. Jeanne most definitely would love heading up the New York office. After what she had just won, she'd even donate Bella to her, she thought magnanimously.

"I guessed right," Kane murmured contentedly later, when pulling the sheet over them. "I needed only the one change of clothes."

"Mmm?" Ellen asked sleepily.

"Hush," he whispered as he settled her head onto his shoulder with a sigh of satisfaction. "I'll explain it tomorrow, when we're on the plane."

the end